And You Came Along
By
Elaine Stock

I0537764

And You Came Along by Elaine Stock

© 2017 Elaine Stock

Published by GTG Publishing

ISBN: 978-0-9995763-0-4

This novella is a work of fiction. Any mention of real events, businesses, organizations, and locales is intended to give the fiction a sense of reality. Names of characters, incidents, and dialogue are solely the product of the author's imagination and creativity and are not expected to be real. Any resemblance to actual persons, living or dead, is entirely coincidental.

Cover Design by Elaine Stock and Norma Budden.

<u>Endorsements for *And You Came Along*</u>:

In Elaine Stock's heartwarming story of hope and second chances, two people discover that God often works in mysterious ways as they learn the past doesn't define them. Her characters will steal your heart, particularly little Caleb. - **Patricia Bradley** author of *Matthews Choice* and the *Christmas Campaign* from Harlequin Heartwarming and *The Logan Point Series* and *The Memphis Cold Case Novels*.

I loved this story! Jacey and Zander each have real challenges presented and it takes something unexpected to bring them together at just the right moment. The kindness of strangers reinforces the subtle undertone of Christmas miracles. A warm, romantic novella perfect not only for Christmas, but also year round! – **Tammy Doherty**, award-winning author of *She's Mine, Celtic Knot, Claddaugh, Celtic Cross*.

Elaine Stock brought me right into her story. I felt I was a part of it from the first paragraph. My heart broke for Jacey, as it looked like her world was falling apart piece by piece. Then we meet Zander, life hasn't been easy for him lately either. Definitely read *And You Came Along* to see if these two can overcome an obstacle they both didn't see coming their way. - **Jann W. Martin**, Teacher, speaker, blogger and Award-winning author of *This Babe So Small* and the *Bible Characters Through the Ages Series*.

Fall in love with charming characters and a story line that will keep you turning the pages. *And You Came Along* is a sweet second chance romance that will warm your heart and soul. - **Cindy Patterson**, award-winning inspirational romance author of *Chasing Paradise* and *Broken Butterfly*.

<u>Acknowledgments</u>

TO MY HOLY FATHER, may this story glorify You.

To my best friend, my husband, Wally. Thanks for believing that true love is never mistaken.

A big thank you to Patricia Bradley, Tammy Doherty, Jann W. Martin, and Cindy Patterson for wanting to read Jacey and Zander's story and for your endorsements.

Thank you to all the sweet members of my Avenue E Street Team. You ladies are wonderful and I can't imagine releasing this novella without you.

To Terri Clark for suggesting the name of Samson for my dog.

To Tom Threadgill, of Eagle Eye Edits, for the superb editing.

Chapter 1

Jacey Tucker shoved open the red-and-green tinsel-decorated doors of Rick's Diner and nearly barreled into an exiting elderly couple. Peggy and Tom, two regulars at the Kindred Lake, Pennsylvania, dining hot spot. Her heart pounded at the near miss. This depressing day was moving quickly from bad to worse.

"Pardon me." She tightened her grip on four-year-old Caleb's hand.

"Oh, you're fine." Peggy patted Caleb's cheek and glanced at Jacey. "My, you look troubled, dear."

With a fixed smile in place, Jacey held back the truth clogging her throat. "It'll be okay. You two have a great day." She stepped aside as the couple exited into the frigid, blustery morning.

Peggy and Tom might have a nice day, but her own odds were pretty slim. By this time on a normal Tuesday her son would be at the church's preschool and she'd be buzzing around the diner serving hungry customers. The notice she'd received in the mail, the one now sizzling in her coat pocket, changed everything.

Caleb covered his ears. "Mama, the music's loud. Everyone's loud."

Jacey lowered his hands. "Hold on, pumpkin. It'll be quieter when we go in the kitchen."

Her son was right, though. Between the easy listening radio station blasting Christmas tunes from the corner stereo speakers and the gabby breakfast crowd hyped on coffee, the volume was high. She just hoped her boss's reaction to her news didn't exceed the restaurant's decibels.

Waitresses swirled around the tables like ballerinas in the Nutcracker suite. The aromas of cheesy egg omelets, sweet maple syrup, and fried bacon drifted through the restaurant and flopped Jacey's empty belly.

Caleb wiggled free from her hand. "Too tight."

"Sorry, sweetie." Her son was the only one she could cling to these days. She drew an imaginary heart on his chest with her index finger. "Here's a great big heart 'cause I love you."

Her little guy giggled.

"Hey, Jacey." Mandy, a co-worker, stopped before them. The redhead balanced a tray of three dishes overflowing with pancakes and fruit-topped waffles. She flashed a sideways smile at Caleb. "Hi, cutie."

Caleb's eyes widened and he pointed to her head. "You got a fuzzy Santa hat. I want one."

Jacey shook her head. "Another time—"

Mandy slid off the festive garment and plopped it on Caleb. The big hat sagged and rode his tiny shoulders like a cape. "Know what you can say to folks?"

Caleb beamed. "Ho ho ho."

"You're such a smart boy." Mandy looked at Jacey, worry lines wrinkling her brow. "Better see Rick. He's pretty ticked at your no-show."

"Well, he's going to have to understand."

Mandy rolled her eyes. "Yeah, right."

"Where is he?"

"Out back." Mandy jutted her chin at a booth packed tight with five men. "Gotta go."

"Sure, see you later." She could only hope this messy situation would pass and she'd work beside her friend later.

Caleb worked his coat zipper up and down. "Can we go home?"

Home.

Her belly twisted again. "Let's find Rick first."

She held her breath in expectation that Caleb's patience remained strong . . . and her boss's too. After peering through the kitchen door's window to check for exiting traffic, she knew she couldn't delay the inevitable any further. "Caleb, want to help push the door open?"

A sweet grin lit his face. He loved this game and they'd played it often during his frequent visits. He stuck his arm out. "One, two, three."

They inched forward in the one direction she didn't want to go. Five men, including Rick, buzzed about as they fried, grilled, scooped, and plated food, making small guy-talk. Then, as if Jacey had cast a spell on them, silence spread from one worker to another as they noticed her and Caleb. Rick jabbed the boom box, deadening the frantic hard rock music. The quiet combined with the harsh white lighting made her wobbly. The questioning stares didn't help.

Rick pushed away from a center prep area, a giant mound of chopped carrots before him. His steely gray eyes darkened and he placed the knife on the cutting board.

"I can explain." The words gushed from Jacey's mouth, though no others followed. She'd mentally rehearsed exactly what she would say to her boss, but as she studied the man's grim expression, reasoning failed her.

Rick wiped his hands on the apron wrapped around his slim waist. For a cook who constantly tasted his creations, he'd managed to avoid packing on the middle-age pounds. Jacey wished he looked more like a jolly round Santa. One with the kind, gentle face she needed.

She swallowed dryly. Christmas, with all its fond memories of celebrating, might very well be making an appearance in five calendar days, but the way life was going it might as well be five months from now. She glanced at Caleb. Her poor boy. It was looking more like no *fa la la* holiday for him either.

Rick hurried away from the prep area and loomed before her, his scowl all the evidence she needed as to which way the conversation was heading.

The door crashed open as Mandy and another server burst into the kitchen.

"Table five's griping about the wait," the older waitress said.

Mandy flashed a little smile at Jacey then hung another order on the clip over the serving counter. "And my group of ten bottomless pits have decided they're not full enough." She sighed. "Get those eggs cracking."

A discordant melody of clangs and claps ensued as the men hustled to get the food out. Rick motioned for Jacey and Caleb to step to the side. He ordered the guys to keep hopping with the food orders.

"You always manage to dish out explanations and this one better be good." He pointed toward the door separating the packed dining area from the white and metallic silver kitchen then squeezed his mouth into a thin line. "You were supposed to be here at seven. We've had one crowd after another out there. We could have used you."

"I picked up my mail." She cringed, aware of how lame she sounded.

Caleb righted the lopsided red felt hat. "Mama got Christmas stamps."

Rick smiled. "Nice hat, Mr. Santa. Eric is making a yummy dessert. Go on over. I bet he'll give you a taste."

A thin, ponytailed man, barely more than a teenager, waved from the pastry workstation in the corner. "Come on over, pal. I'm making chocolate pudding pie."

Jacey's breathing eased as her son trotted toward the friendly guy. The joy of her little boy's growing independence stopped there as she again faced her boss. To his credit, he didn't cross his arms. He wasn't naturally intimidating, but every business owner had a limit. She licked her dry lips. "I received unexpected news today."

He glanced at the wall clock. "It took you three hours to chill from it?"

Her hands shook. The paper she'd slipped from her pocket dropped to the tiled floor. She retrieved the notice and it almost dropped again from her sweaty hand. She opened her mouth to explain, but Rick cut her off with a shake of his head.

"I've bought into enough of your excuses. An ill mom. Apartment hopping. A broken-down car. What is it today?"

She waved the morning's freshly delivered bad news like a white flag of surrender. "Listen, Rick. Please. This is an eviction notice. Caleb and I need to find a new home. Fast, like today or tomorrow tops. I need a few days off."

"A few days off? During the holiday season? Our busiest time of the year?"

A chill pricked her arms and she shivered. "It's not my fault."

"I'm going to have to let you go. I have a business to operate. You know I don't expect anything more from my staff than I demand of myself. I work seven days a week and more than twelve-hour shifts despite the personal stuff happening in my life."

She craned her neck to check on Caleb. He'd just followed Eric into the walk-in cooler. Out of earshot. "But I have a child to take care of . . . and now no home."

Rick grimaced. "Go back to your family."

She lowered her head. Her stepdad's squinty eyes flashed before her. Angry heat flushed her face. "If I could, don't you think I would?"

"Hey, Rick," one of the guys called. "It's Christmas, man. Have a heart."

Without turning around, Rick lifted a brow. "I do have a heart. I'll arrange for your next paycheck to have a little more than your usual. Sorry, things might be different if you didn't have a history of this stuff, but I can't be taken advantage of. Best of luck." He sped into the dining room.

She looked up as her fellow co-workers offered commiserative words. Her *former* co-workers.

"Thanks guys." She dropped her chin. "I'm going to miss you."

Caleb ran out to her, a dollop of chocolate smudged on the corner of his lip.

She grasped his hand. "Time to go. Say . . ." Her breath caught. Hot tears brimmed her eyes. She waved at the guys, too choked to speak sad words.

"Bye-bye," Caleb said. "Are we going home?"

"I'll figure it out in a moment, buddy." She bent over to zip his thrift-store-bargain coat, which he was growing fast out of. Her nose twitched as she inhaled his strawberry-scented baby shampoo. Before this awful day her son always helped her to forget her troubles. Daily she thanked God for this blessing of joy, her son. Without one last peek over her shoulder at the kitchen crew, she scurried from the room. Maybe an eviction notice wasn't quite a death sentence, but its initial sting earlier this morning had steamrolled over her. One way or the other, she needed to rise above this difficult situation.

Hand in hand with her son, she stepped outdoors. A blast of wind slashed at her cheeks, further strengthening her resolve. They'd survived on their own this long, and now she'd find a way for them to thrive. She squeezed her child's hand. "Ready for an adventure?"

Caleb nodded and stretched his hand out, palm up. "Look, Mama. It's snowing."

ZANDER PAXTON TOSSED the last of the two duffel bags into the Jeep Cherokee's rear as the first flakes floated down. Looked like the forecasters were spot-on with their predictions. Good thing the call was for only a couple of inches, and restricted to northern Maryland. He and his co-pilot, Samson, should be able to navigate the three-hour drive from Baltimore to Kindred Lake without a major problem. Tag on another hour if he needed to slow down due to the snow, or if he or Samson needed a john break. No sweat. His parents certainly managed the miles plenty of times when visiting him. A little weather blip sure wasn't going to keep him from seeing them, especially since their arrangements now included a lengthy stay. And if he needed a reminder of how determined he could be, all he needed to do was look at his recovery over the past few months.

He whistled for Samson. The black-and-white Border collie came running at full speed from around the corner of the house and brushed against Zander's jeans-clad legs. "Ready, boy?" He bent to rub between the dog's ears. Muscle spasms seared through his lower back, right where the bullet had ripped into him six months ago. His hand slid from Samson. Winded, he bent over bracing both his hands on his knees. He gritted his teeth as sweat formed on his brow. No way. Not going to accept the pain.

As if reading his mind, Samson barked, cheering him along. Zander willed himself to stand. And he did. Slow, but surely.

"Samson, did you do your business? It's a long ride, pal."

The collie yipped and his tail became a side-to-side blur.

"All right, then. Let's go." He favored his right hip as he made his way to the passenger side and opened the door for Samson to leap in. He then crossed to the driver's side with his hands shoved into his jacket pockets to avoid the temptation to use the hood as a handrail.

He could do this. He must do this.

One foot in front of the other. Step by step.

Once behind the wheel he cranked up the volume of the radio as a Beethoven sonata began. As he looked into his rearview mirror and backed out of his parking spot in front of his cousin Greg's house, he flashed back to the time when his cuz brought him home from the hospital as a temporary housemate. Greg couldn't stop razzing him about his *sissy* music. "No chick is gonna want a guy who listens to classical music." Didn't matter, he'd told Greg. No gal in her right mind was going to want him in his present, and permanent, new shape.

As he pulled onto Sycamore Lane one particular woman came to mind, forever embedded in his memory as bright, bold and beautiful. He gripped the wheel tighter. He was moving on. He'd never disappoint anyone again. He fixed his attention on the road before him. No more looking back. Best to focus on the future and hope for something—anything—better.

Chapter 2

Caleb kicked the back of Jacey's seat. "Mama, are we on the 'venture yet?"

Jacey glanced into the rearview mirror. Her son had already unzipped his brown corduroy coat. His gray and blue plaid flannel shirt peeked out between the straps of his harness car seat. His adorable ways zinged her with joy. She sniffled. God would see them through their current difficult circumstances. They'd make it, somehow. "You bet we're on our adventure. You'll like my friend Amy. She can't wait to meet you."

"Is that who you called before we left?"

Years had slipped by since she'd last seen her former college roommate, but her friend was still easy to talk to, and had listened sympathetically while Jacey shared her whole sob story. Amy had invited her and Caleb to camp out in her spare bedroom as long as necessary.

"Yes, Amy's who I phoned." She grimaced at the snow caking her windshield wipers and turned the defroster on high. What was up with this weather? This old car, with her nearly bald tires, better make it the thousand plus mile-distance. "And she lives in sunny Florida, a nice and warm place."

"Is that where we're going?"

"We are. Florida is where Mickey Mouse lives, and there are lots of beaches to build sandcastles." She gulped. A fantasy park and beach fun. It sounded so sweet and casual, not as if they were fleeing out of desperation. "We're only staying with Amy until we find me a new job. But she has three boys—triplets—and you'll have lots of fun."

"How come I don't have brothers?"

Jacey's chest grew heavy. She needed to shift the conversation and pushed out his favorite song, "Old Macdonald Had a Farm." He joined in, putting aside the sibling question, for now. Somewhere between miles seven and ten the fun of singing about the old farmer became old news. "Hey, Pumpkin. Want to play 'name the colors' with me?"

"Yeah. You go first, Mama."

She glanced to her left and right. Heavier snow than originally predicted was fast blanketing everything. She warned herself not to panic. "Brown. I see a brown fence."

Caleb swooshed his head back and forth. "I don't see a fence."

She cringed at the expansive white countryside. "Your turn."

"Red. Stop sign."

She gasped. The stop sign she'd just ignored. She stomped on the brake. The car fishtailed right then left then right again before she remembered to take her foot off the brake as well as the accelerator. The car straightened. Fortunately, she was only going thirty miles per hour and no one else was crossing through the intersection.

Her palms burned from the tight grip on the wheel.

"You did it, Mama. You made the car go straight."

"Yes, I did." Sweat broke out across her back. "But now Mama needs to really, really pay attention to her driving. Tell you what. I'll put on a CD for you to listen to. Okay, love?"

Caleb nodded. Jacey slid the children's recording into the player and returned her attention to the road, trying not to succumb to the hypnotic whoosh whoosh of the windshield wipers coming on intermittently. Where were the plow trucks when you needed them? This snail's pace would take them forever to get to Florida, the land of less wintry days and the possibility of less expensive living, which suited her non-existent budget. She fingered the cross around her neck for the briefest of seconds before fixing both hands on the wheel again.

"Mama?"

"Hmm, honey?"

"I was talking. About the snow."

She smiled into the mirror, hoping her son would notice. "Sorry. My ears were napping. What did you say?"

Caleb giggled. "Ears don't nap. You're silly, Mama."

The light tease warmed her insides. "What's up, goose?"

"It's white out. I can't see anything. How much longer to Florida?"

She choked back a sigh. It wasn't Caleb's patience she needed to be concerned about, but rather her own diminishing composure. "Just a little while."

With each mile they crawled, there were less and less vehicles on the road. At least a couple of hours had already passed. One good thing.

"Mama, where are we?"

"We're near the town of New Freedom." Prophetic? Maybe. Hopefully. "We're about to cross into Maryland."

"I'm hungry."

"Want a PBJ?"

He nodded.

"It's in my tote bag, by you. Can you reach it?"

"No. Can you get it?"

She surveyed the road that was taking them through a stretch of houses. The snow was coming down at a good clip, but she'd developed a decent feel for driving in this weather. Besides, only one other vehicle was approaching but it was still a ways off. She could pull off to the side of the road, but with her luck the car would get stuck in the snow. Could she get her son to wait for lunch? Not really. She'd have to slow down, grope around back, find the tote of food, and haul it to the front passenger seat. Bingo, lunchtime.

The car swerved toward the shoulder.

"Mama . . ."

Don't brake. Keep foot off of gas pedal. You've done this once. You'll do it again.

But she jerked the wheel left.

"Mama . . . make the car stop spinning."

The headlights of the oncoming car that seconds ago appeared quite distant struck her eyes from mere feet away.

No. She couldn't let this happen. "Please, Father. Protect Caleb and—"

Chapter 3

Z ander had reduced his speed as soon as he crossed into Pennsylvania and the road conditions worsened. As he entered New Freedom and started to pass the group of houses and saw the oncoming vehicle, he slowed more. Headlights hit his eyes. The Jeep slid. He turned toward the skid. Not working. The world spun. Reflexively, he shot out his arm to hold back Samson. The dog yipped.

"Easy, pal."

Zander's breath hitched. The other car propelled its way closer to him like a rocket. Oh no. No . . . no . . .

Out of the corner of his eye he swore he saw a little boy with a bug-eyed look and a mouth suspended open . . . in a scream? The other driver struck the front left corner of his car. He spun even closer to the other vehicle.

No way was he going to crash again and risk injuring a child. He yanked the wheel a hard right and smacked into two metal trashcans on a curbside. With a jerk to the wheel he was back on the road but slipping fast . . . toward a tree. He couldn't stop. He shot forward. An explosion of heat and pain seared across his face. The airbag. The car tilted on its left wheels before orienting itself and dropping hard, jarring his spine.

Black surrounded him. Was he in heaven or stuck in his vehicle? Wasn't there a kid . . . somewhere? A whimper reached his ears.

Samson.

"Buddy?" Was his pal hurt? Dying? What would he do without his dog?

Why was it dark? And quiet, except for the pinging against . . . his windshield? Ice falling. Definitely explained the terrible road condition.

Heavy movement wiggled across his chest. A warm slimy roughness swiped his cheek.

He cracked open an eye. Samson rested across his upper torso, whining into his ear.

"Good boy." He tried to hug the dog, but couldn't move. No. Not another injury to his back. The doc had warned him that if there was a next time, it might spell permanent paralysis.

One by one, he tested the movement of fingers, toes, hands, and legs. Head, side to side. Eyes open and shut and open. Slowly, the blurriness in his vision faded.

"I'm alive," he said aloud, more for his own sake than Samson's. He sucked in a long breath in dread, poking the animal and hoping he wouldn't cry in pain from an injury. The dog's excitable panting filled his ears instead. A wonderful thing.

A child. In another car. It was coming back to him. He had to help.

Zander jerked upright, smacking his head on the wheel. He'd live. Fresh air would help to tune out the flares of pain igniting his lower back. He propped onto an elbow. In hopes the key was in place, he stretched his hand to the ignition. The remote grazed his fingertips. He turned the key just enough to power down the window a couple of inches, amazed it worked.

A cold mist hit his face, but he could handle the temperature. At least they weren't wedged against a snowbank.

He drew his legs up and over to the door and kicked it open. "Go, buddy." Samson barked and shot out.

It was his turn. There was a boy to check upon, let alone the child's dad or mom or whoever was driving the car. Zander stood, surprised the pain he'd experienced minutes ago failed to shred him into pieces. Adrenaline had its perks.

He shielded his eyes from the snow falling fast and furiously. To his right was a house. Through the whiteout conditions he could barely make out the rooftop of another building across the way. An old barn?

His gaze then took in his smashed vehicle and he winced. Good thing he'd mailed out his car insurance bill early. Samson barked, hauling Zander's attention back to the road and a small cherry-red sedan a few yards from his, sitting still as death. He did something he hadn't done in months. He ran, managing to keep his balance on the slippery pavement.

With a pound on the driver's window, he gave a shout. "Hey, can you hear me? I'm here to help."

Chloe's warm eyes flashed before him. He'd failed to protect his partner and a life was lost. Because of him. Not again. Not if he could help it.

This time he banged a fist against the rear passenger window. "You okay?"

He wiped the snow off the window with his bare hand and peered in. A little boy was slumped to the side, jammed in one of those child car seats. A Santa hat hung crookedly off his head. Movement to the left hauled his attention to the front seat. The driver. He looked into the driver's window. A woman, strewn on her side, looked blankly ahead.

He grasped the door handle. Locked.

Chapter 4

The black faded to a gray fog then thinned to white edges as Jacey fluttered her lashes. "Caleb," she called. Forget herself, the car, or the details of what happened. Her only concern was her son.

No reply came. She groped around her sides and shrieked. "Baby, baby, where are you? Talk to me, Caleb."

She tried to sit up, but couldn't move. Something pinned her in place. Unless she was hurt. No. *Don't think about my needs. Just get to my little sweetie.*

Two sounds reached her at the same time. Tapping. Whimpering.

"Caleb?"

"Mama. I'm scared."

He was alive. Thank you, God. Thank you, God. Thank you, God.

"Come here, sweetheart."

Silence. Was he nodding or shaking his head? "Talk in words, baby."

"The belt on my tummy's tight. I can't move."

The belt must have pulled tight if he was thrust forward. Is that why he sounded short of breath? She should have insisted he remove his bulky coat before they started the drive. Stupid old car. Stupid bad heater.

More tapping came, this time frantic.

"Look, Mama."

If he was pointing, she couldn't see the direction or the object of his attention. For that matter, she couldn't move her head. Panic jabbed at her insides. She was going to freak out.

No. Think of Caleb. You're his mommy.

Tap. Tap. A shout.

"Mama, the man's yelling at us."

A man?

"I see you in there. Are you hurt? Can you hear me?"

A man was indeed shouting.

Caleb was crying.

A dog barked.

She blinked, pushing away hysteria. "Hello?"

"Don't move," the stranger said. "You may do harm. I'm getting help."

"Don't leave us." But no sound other than her son's cries filled her ears. She tried to lift her head, but fell back the inches she'd accomplished.

"Where did the man go, Mama?"

Good. Caleb was talking. She needed to keep him alert and calm. Herself too.

"Can you see outside the car, honey?"

"I see a house."

"Tell me about the house. What does it look like?"

"It's white, and big. But everything's white. 'Cause of the snow."

"What do you see?"

"The door's open. I see a man. And a doggy."

"What else do you see, hon?"

"I'm cold, Mama. Why's it cold?"

"The car isn't running to make us warm. But, soon we'll be nice and toasty. Can you wait like a big boy?"

"Yes." The one word fell from his mouth in broken pieces. Not good.

"Sweetheart, what else do you—"

"Mama, the man is coming back. Two men."

A tap came against the window glass. "Miss, I'm here with help. Hold tight. We'll get you out."

The car shook. She swallowed back a wave of queasiness.

"Mama, they're opening the door."

She concentrated on Caleb. "Don't be afraid. They'll help us."

Metal clanged and groaned. Cold air plowed into the car.

A silver-haired man wearing a thick blue parka appeared before her. "We got in, Ma'am. My name's Joe Billings. You and this fellow, Zander, were in a car accident. We'll help you and the boy get into a warmer place."

"He's my son, Caleb." Cars about to collide flashed in her mind. She swallowed hard. "Zander? Is he okay?"

"Just fine." A man, around her age, inched closer into her limited area of view. A missing smile and wrinkled brow countered his warm brown eyes. Red scratches on his cheeks notched up her concern of his own injuries from the accident.

"Ma'am?" Joe said. "Can you tell me . . ."

She started to shake.

"We'll get you plenty warm in no time. Tell me your name."

"Jacey."

"Good. I'm glad to see—"

"Where are we?"

"You're near the Maryland border. Let's get you indoors and I'll call my friends on the ambulance squad for medical advice."

"I'm sore, but I'll be fine." She glanced about. "My son? Is he hurt?"

Joe smiled at her. "I'm no doctor, but he seems fine. Shaken, but that's understandable. Zander just unbuckled him from his seat. The harness strap appears to have cinched around his middle a bit on the hard side. No apparent injuries, but it would be best to watch for signs of internal damage."

She gasped.

Joe patted her shoulder. "We have him tucked under a blanket, but he's active and chatting away with Zander. Great signs. It's you we're concerned about. Apparently, the air bag failed to deploy." He pointed at her. "Like Zander, you also have scratches to your face. I'm worried about broken bones and a concussion, but like I said, I'm no medic or doctor. Shouldn't speak prematurely."

She swallowed back rising panic. "Why can't I move?"

"You're trapped under seat parts and a few belongings that flew on top of you. Zander and I are going to lift them off, but if it's painful let us know right away and I'll phone for an ambulance first. I'm just concerned since it's a volunteer company that they can't mobilize in this awful blizzard. But let's take it step-by-step."

"Blizzard?"

"Yes. The storm's been upgraded to a blizzard. A good two feet is predicted, and that's minimally. It's not supposed to stop until tomorrow afternoon. The roads south of town are closed. They've warned all non-essential vehicles to stay put." Joe cleared his throat. "Hate to say it, but if you're not hurt, other than the possible loss of your car, it looks like luck stopped you from continuing on with your journey and getting into a more horrid situation." Joe glanced over his shoulder. "And you as well, Zander."

The younger man returned to her side. "I don't believe in luck these days, but I'm relieved to have met you."

"My wife, Aubrey, and I will do what we can to make the three of you comfortable and safe." Joe lifted a headrest, a children's book, and a dented infant car seat carrier off Jacey. "Tell me there's no baby onboard."

She shook her head. "No. My son and I, that's all. I never got around to cleaning out the car."

Joe softly chuckled. "You're sounding better." He signaled to Zander. "Now, let's help you sit, nice and slowly, and see about getting you out of this mess."

Joe reached for her left hand; Zander grasped her right shoulder. A wave of comfort warmed her, at least for the briefest of seconds until Caleb complained he was cold.

She sat upright, relieved no black dots paraded before her eyes. "I'm good. No horrible aches. I broke my arm years ago and remember well what busted bones feel like."

"Think you're ready to stand?" Joe asked.

"I'm still cold, Mama."

She looked at her son. He'd climbed over the seat and now pressed against her side. "There's my answer. I'm definitely ready to get me and Caleb out and into a warmer place."

Caleb slipped the blanket off of his shoulders. "Want to use this?"

Zander helped to cover him again. "Hey, buddy. I have another one for your mommy. You wear this and she'll wear hers." He slipped a gray wool blanket around Jacey. When he went to secure it shut by her throat, his hand brushed against hers. Warmth jumped from his fingers to hers. They locked gazes.

"She's not my mommy," Caleb said, drawing everyone's attention. "She's Mama."

Jacey reached to muss Caleb's hair and cringed.

Zander bent closer to her face. "What's wrong?"

"Just sore."

"You will be for a while," Joe said. "Let's move you two out of this car and into a warm place and make it all better."

All better. At least until the snow ended and the roads cleared. As soon as possible she'd rent a car and continue to Amy's. The more miles between them and Kindred Lake the better. Nothing would stop them.

Chapter 5

Outside of the car, a gust of wind shoved against Jacey's back and with hands extended out, she stopped herself from falling against the vehicle. Her legs wobbled.

"Whoa," Zander said as he reached for her. "I gotcha." Though she still was wrapped within the blanket, Zander slipped off his jacket and placed it on her shoulders. He pulled her tighter to his side. Bitter cold continued to lash its fury at them. "Extra help against this nasty temperature."

With his arm around her waist his warmth snuggled up to her. Nice, but awkward. He might be helping her, but she didn't know this guy and tried to pull away.

His grasp tightened around her middle. "Not so fast. I don't want you to fall."

"Honestly, I'm fine." She pointed at what used to be her car. "That's why I'm shaky."

"Understandable. My car isn't in better shape." He glanced down the road. "Having our cars towed to a garage doesn't look to be happening soon. I'm more concerned about getting us out of this storm and into safety. Joe's offer of his guest cabin sounds like an invite to a resort right now."

Ahead of them, Zander's dog bounded through the piling snow as Joe trudged across his snow-covered lawn while carrying her son toward the house. A bright light over the front door shined like a beacon of warmth and hope, a promise of safety waiting inside. Her little boy had accurately described the old colonial farmhouse as big. She imagined the place with its lovely porch, green window shutters, and two brick chimneys on its ends, appeared charming each season. But, she didn't see any other building on the property. "Guest cabin?"

"His wife is ill with the flu and they don't want to make us sick. The cabin is behind the house and a little up a hill. Joe says it has everything we need."

Jacey made her way to the curb. She studied her boots, at least the little of them that wasn't buried in the snow. "How many bedrooms?"

"One. Not a problem. You and your son can have it. I'll take the couch. Don't worry, I'm a true gentleman."

She didn't know him from any other stranger, but his kind smile indicated she could trust him. There was a storm raging on. It wasn't like she had a choice.

He gestured toward the front door of the Billings' house. Joe stood outside, blankets bundled under one arm and a brown grocery sack nestled in the other. "Let's grab the essentials we can from our cars and get indoors."

She rubbed her hands. "Good idea. I can barely feel my fingers."

Jacey managed to salvage only one of Caleb's storybooks and her purse from the buried mess. She sighed a frustrated groan.

Zander patted her arm. "All that counts right now is we're alive and have managed to get stuck at the doorstep of nice folks."

She nodded. He was right. It could have been far worse. She peered upwards and whispered her thanks to God. When she turned back to Zander, one brow was lifted. "Not into amens?"

"Ready?"

A cold, emptiness bounced within her. Her faith had carried her through much anguish and would get her through this passing situation. She wanted to ask what helped him during tough times, but the freezing outdoors wasn't a place to talk. "Got what you need?"

"Just grabbed a duffel and supplies for Samson." He took her arm again and they plodded through the snowdrifts toward the house.

She slipped twice, but he was quick to straighten her. Just short of
Joe's front door, Zander lurched forward. Just as fast, he jerked his torso
upright. A stamp of pain marched across his face as he hissed a sharp in-
take of breath into her ear.

"Zander?"

He waved her off with his free hand. "Fine. Spasm."

Caleb stepped out from the house. "Mama, hurry." A cozy yellow
light backlit him and made him appear as if he were center stage. Well,
he was. The center stage of her heart.

"I'm getting there, pumpkin."

"It's nice here. There's a big Christmas tree. We can't stay inside 'cause
Mrs. Joe's sick. And there's a cat. It's orange. Joe says his name is Thomas.
The cat likes Zander's dog."

Joe placed a hand on her son's shoulder. "Aubrey agrees you're wel-
come to use the guest cabin for as long as needed. We built it a few years
ago for when our growing family or friends visit. It's small but cozy and
has plenty of bedding and guest supplies. And I'll bring food as quick as I
can. About the only things you'll notice missing are TV and bonuses like
a hot tub and dishwasher."

"Won't miss them." Jacey opened her arms and motioned to Caleb.
He arrowed right to her and threw his arms around her middle. "Thank
you, Joe, for the hospitality."

"That's very accommodating," Zander said. "Thanks."

"Take this flashlight. If you don't mind, I want to check on Aubrey."
Joe handed Jacey the light. "Watch your step in the snow."

"Of course. You stay with your wife. We will manage fine."

Zander reached for her hand. "We're in this together. We'll work it
out."

Jacey glanced at their linked hands. For the craziest of seconds, she
didn't want to let go.

Chapter 6

Jacey's gaze roamed the cabin. It might have been small, with only one main room with an eat-in kitchen, a bedroom, and a bath, but it was comfy. Old daguerreotypes of funny hunting scenes hanging from its pine walls, braided rugs, and little country chic touches scattered throughout, like wooden-carved butterflies and five bear cubs captured in playful poses made the place enchanting. Tucked under a red wool blanket for the past hour with Caleb on the brown-and-white plaid sofa, she stretched. A stab of pain poked her side, but considering the potential of harm from the car accident as well as the storm, she counted her blessings. It could have been far worse. She ran her fingers through her son's hair. "This place is nice, isn't it?" He nodded against her side, attention fixed on his storybook.

A rap came at the door.

She glanced up to catch Zander signal from the kitchen table that he'd greet the caller. Samson followed his master.

"Hi, Joe. Let me help you." Zander took a big casserole dish from the smiling man.

Joe stamped the snow from his boots then leaned against the shut door. "It is plain brrr out there. Glad you folks are inside safe and sound."

"Understatement." Jacey stood fast, her hips and back rebelled and begged to rest. Instead, she padded shoeless to the entrance. Without thinking twice she rose on her toes and kissed the older man's cheek. "Thanks again, Joe. We'd be lost without you and Aubrey. And you shouldn't have shortchanged this lovely cabin earlier when you described it to us." She waved her hands. "I love this place."

"Thanks. I'll be sure and tell Aubrey. That will cheer her up a bit." Joe lifted the tote and jutted his chin toward the dish Zander held. "Speaking of, if Aubrey had to become ill with the flu, her timing was good right before the storm started. Our neighbors from down the road dropped off more casseroles, soups, and stews than our fridge and freezer can handle. Name it and there's plenty of it. Aubrey insists we share it with you."

Jacey eyed the casserole dish, hoping her stomach wouldn't growl in betrayal. "But it was meant for you two."

"If I bring one teaspoon back, I'm a goner." Joe winked. "Aubrey already warned me to keep the three of you fed and happy. There's ziti, baguettes, and dessert. Tomorrow morning I'll bring you over breakfast."

"I like Cheerios," Caleb announced from the sofa.

"You got it. On top of the fresh eggs from our chickens and muffins pulled from Aubrey's freezer." Joe looked at Zander. "Any trouble with the woodstove?"

"No, sir. Jacey did an awesome job making it nice and warm."

Joe's eyes widened and he tilted his head toward Jacey.

Jacey hugged her middle. "My stepdad, um, kept his distance while I was growing up, but he did share his secrets for successful fires."

"Good for him." Joe set the tote on the narrow kitchen table beside the picture window. "Aubrey says to keep the ziti covered with the tinfoil while you heat it up. Enjoy. Have a good night."

"Night night, Mr. Joe," Caleb called.

By the door again, Joe faced the boy. "You, young man, are a keeper. Your mom's blessed to have you as her son." He hurried out the door as Jacey and Zander exchanged goodnights with him.

As she took a step toward the kitchen, a sudden wave of exhaustion rocked Jacey dizzy. Her belly flip-flopped and she gripped the back of a recliner for support. The room spun and she plopped into the chair.

In a flash, Zander stood beside her. "Hey. What's wrong?"

With tangled words jamming her mouth, she only managed to shake her head.

Chapter 7

Zander reached out to touch Jacey's shoulder. "Is your head hurting? I'll go see if I can borrow aspirin from Joe. Dinner might—"

She lifted a hand and shook her head. "The day's just catching up with me. I'll be fine."

He studied her. Yeah, right. She'd be fine like her banged-up car would straighten out the dents and cracks by itself. He rubbed his hand across his chest and inhaled deeply. She's troubled, stranded away from home in the middle of a storm, and has a child to look after. He'd be upset too. And this woman, pretty as she was with those lake-blue eyes and a soft-complexioned face with all the cute looks at all the right times, stabbed at him in a way he couldn't explain. Her combo of smarts and vulnerability didn't hurt either.

"That's great news," he said, aiming for a bit of levity. "I'll level with you, but don't tell my buddies. I freak if a woman cries. Unhinged me is not a pretty picture."

A sound gushed from her bow-shaped lips. Oh, man. She's going to bawl.

She moved her head an inch. Wait a second. Her lips lifted and a chuckle bubbled out. A sweet sound. Relief flooded him.

"You freak? I may like seeing that."

He pulled a ladder-back chair from the kitchen table, dragged it beside her, and then saddled it, resting his arms against the top rung. "You into crazy guys?"

She laughed more heartily. Her wheat-blonde hair framed her face and accented those awesome eyes.

He nodded. "Definitely better. Laughing is a good thing, even at me."

She raked her fingers through her hair and brushed tresses away from her face. "Actually, tame and friendly is more my thing. You come off as..." She tapped her chin with a fingertip.

"Manly? Hunky?" He winked at her. "Oh, come on. Say it. I come off as Mr. Virile, right out of every woman's fantasy."

She laughed hard, wrapping her arms around her slim waist as if she was about to explode. And the thing was, he laughed right along with her, unable to stop. They sounded good together.

She simmered down first. "Thanks."

"For what, Jacey?"

A little smile tugged at her lips. "For smoothing the edges of a really awful day." She looked past him at her son on the couch. Wide-awake a few minutes ago, he was now snoozing like a baby lamb. His arm was draped off the side with his outstretched fingers touching the napping Samson.

The kid made him smile. He was adorable, and smart too. Children usually didn't remain on his radar, but Caleb zinged Zander's attention like no other, reminding him of the laughs he and his dad had shared on walks and backyard campouts. "He's definitely a cute one."

She patted her heart. "He's my universe."

Zander wanted to reach for her hand. Instead, he rubbed his chin, already scratchy with the day's scruff. He wasn't a natural hand-holder. These days, it was best to steer away from relationships. He shook his head to clear the tumbleweeds skipping through his mind.

"Zander?"

He looked up.

"You have a great name, by the way. Your mom was creative."

He shrugged. "Just a name."

"In my book, everyone's unique. Your mom saw something special in you."

The last time he spoke with his mom broadcasted loud and clear in his mind as if she sat beside him. He loved her, but he needed to hear her doubts over his full recovery as much as he needed to visualize his dim future.

"So tell me about your rotten day."

"You're changing the topic."

"Yep. I'm thinking there's more to this day than winding up trapped in a cabin with a handsome dude." He thumbed his chest. "Cue the handsome dude."

She giggled, then laughed harder.

When was the last time he'd heard a giggle in response to what he'd said? She spurred him to play it up.

"Was it the handsome dude part?"

Her mouth grew small. "The surprise element of landing here, in this cabin."

That was the second true outburst of laughter he'd heard from her. Now it was gone. His instinct was to jump on the table and break out into a standup comic routine, not that he was a pro at jokes. Or crank up the stereo and spin her silly in ancient disco moves, not that there was a stereo in the cabin, though he could definitely manage the bad dancing, especially with his out-of-shape body. Whatever it took to make her smile again.

He rocked back, overcome by a somber gloom. What was he thinking? He didn't know her worth squat. She didn't know him. And he wasn't looking for any changes.

Jacey stood, tested a step, and then went to the table and reached for the sacks of food. "Let me take care of this." She sighed. "I guess if we were going to become marooned, right here with Joe and Aubrey is perfect. Considerate folks. God always does a great job watching over us, though I wish I could remember that more often."

Zander couldn't help but notice her last few words were murmured, as if a reflection. "He quit watching over me a while back."

"Pardon?"

He stood. Fire lashed at his back. A groan escaped his lips.

Immediately, Jacey stood beside him and placed a hand on his arm. "Can I help?"

"Old wound." He willed away the pain, or at least the focus on it. His attention landed at the place above his elbow where her hand rested. "It's nothing. Sat too long."

Her eyes narrowed. She didn't believe him but he wasn't going to spit out the details. For her sake.

She pointed to a grocery bag on the table. "You unpack the bread and dessert goodies. I'll take care of the ziti. You and Caleb may be in stiff competition over the pasta."

He unwrapped the tin foil around the baguette. The tang of sauce, garlic, oregano, and cheese zoomed upward. He inhaled deeply and rubbed at his stomach. "Wow." He turned to get a better look at the food—and Jacey.

A single tear dripped down her cheek. His gut twisted. He had to help.

Chapter 8

Jacey couldn't turn fast enough from Zander to hide the lone tear trickling down her cheek.

He stepped closer. "Ah, my eyes also well with tears when I'm about to feast on Italian food."

She sniffled. He wanted to make her smile again? Why her? It didn't really matter. She wasn't sure if she could dare try to look on the bright side of things again. "Do you always resort to humor?"

"When I'm at a loss of better responses." He rubbed his neck. "I'll handle dinner if you'd like."

She carried the pan of ziti over to the oven, set it on a burner and then set the temperature to 380 degrees.

"Good thing that's a gas oven. Handy if the power goes out."

She glanced over her shoulder and jumped. He'd narrowed the distance between them by mere inches. "You're light on your feet."

He grinned "A necessary trait in my line of work."

"Cat burglary?"

"Like your humor, too."

Jacey placed the hefty pan of food into the oven then leaned against the door. "I have served countless baked ziti dinners to oodles of ravenous customers . . . but it's a bit overwhelming, right this second. I'm kind of whacked up emotionally."

"Are you a chef?"

"Try an unemployed waitress." She veiled her face with her hands. "An unemployed waitress booted out of her apartment without a place to live."

"That's rough. And sad." Zander glanced at Caleb still sound asleep on the couch. Her little one had rolled onto his side. Samson had moved

31

beside his new friend, his head across the boy's lap. "Is Caleb aware of what's happening?"

"He thinks we're on an adventure," she said softly, although her son was a heavy sleeper. "We kind of are. My friend in Florida is generous enough to offer us a couple of beds until I can find my way. Again."

"Hmm. There's that awful word, *again*. I hear you." He jutted out his chin toward the kitchen table and chairs. "Let's sit."

"But your back? Or is it your leg? A few minutes ago you complained about sitting. And I noticed a slight limp earlier."

"It's the faulty body part du jour." He grinned. "I'll have to tell the guys that the lady I was holed up in a cabin with kept a sharp eye on me."

"Yeah, right." They stepped toward the table. He sucked in his breath and she hooked arms with him. "Let me help."

"I'm fine. I can make it on my own."

"And I can help you. Don't fight me." She followed his gaze to their intertwined arms.

"Not used to someone coming to your aid?"

"Let's just say I'm out of practice." He tried to pull away but she held fast.

She stopped a foot short of the table. "Would it be better for you to stand?"

"You ask a lot of questions." He slipped loose of her hold and pulled out a chair. "Just for you."

"You're a headstrong guy, but a gentleman." She sat. "Thanks."

"I've been called worse." He slumped onto his chair, twisting in an unusual way.

"Trying to avoid a tender spot?"

He didn't reply.

"Zander, I hope I'm not prying, but I sense you're also facing some uncertainties."

He scraped his chin against his knuckles, and looked straight ahead. "You're not the only one in search of the next great residence."

She swiped at her eyes. "Oh, I'm sorry to hear that."

"I appreciate it."

She reached to pull her hair back from her face, but stopped when he fixed his gaze on her. She couldn't turn away. Didn't want to. He had the thickest black lashes she'd ever seen on a man. "I hate seeing anyone suffer."

"At least I saw my situation coming. Sounds like you found out about both your job and apartment back-to-back."

She lowered her head. "This morning. Received an eviction notice in the mail."

"Aren't those notices usually served?"

She shrugged.

"Are you late in rent or have you violated the lease conditions?"

"None of the above. Landlord wants me out. Short and not sweet."

"And the creep didn't give you a ten-day notice to look elsewhere?"

"Like I said, he wants me out. Must have someone else in mind for the place. He always seemed like a nice guy until . . ."

"Until today, right?"

"It doesn't matter." She sighed. "It's all past tense now."

"Can you go after him legally for the way he evicted you?"

"Maybe, but I think it's best to move on." She glanced at Caleb. "My son's more important than anyone, thing, or place." She paused, waiting for her emotions to steady. Sentimentality over the bald and unsmiling landlord reminded her a tad of her stepfather. She had to concentrate now on her future. "This whole mess made me late for work this morning at the diner. My boss wasn't in the mood for anymore of my excuses and said bye-bye."

"But Christmas is four days away, if you don't include today."

"Ho ho ho and all that jazz."

"Mama," Caleb called from the sofa. "I was asleep."

"You were, my love."

"I'm hungry." Her little pumpkin rubbed his eyes. "I smell good food. Something I like. Is Samson hungry?"

"Samson has plenty of chow in his dish and fresh water in his bowl." Zander stood and withdrew the last tray of dessert from the bag and peeked under the tin foil covering. "And we have baked ziti, bread, and brownies. I love brownies."

"Zander!" Caleb bounced to his feet and charged toward him. Samson followed, his collar tags jingling. "I dreamed about you. But you're real."

Zander tousled Caleb's sleep-mussed hair. Jacey lifted a brow. Her little boy admired this stranger fast becoming a new friend. The two always had a ready wide smile for each other. She couldn't remember the last time a man had made her little boy happy

"I'm definitely real, buddy."

Jacey smiled to herself. Yep, Zander was indeed real. An odd mixture of sparks and shudders tingled her arms. While she had once hoped to meet a nice guy—like Zander seemed to be—this was the wrong time and wrong place to be thinking about a man. She and Caleb would weather out the storm then get on their way. Zander had his own life to live.

A smile lit Caleb's face. "I'm your buddy?"

"You bet you are."

Caleb tugged at Jacey's sweater. "I'm hungry, Mama. When are we eating?"

"In just a few minutes, hon." She flashed a big smile at her son. "We're having an early dinner today, and afterward we'll relax for a while. Zander wants to play with you until dinner's ready."

Zander scratched his head. "I do?"

"But my toys got hurt in the car." Caleb ran to the window. "It's still snowing. And I don't see nothing."

Zander walked over to him and placed a hand on his shoulder. "Oh, the car's there, Caleb. It's buried under the snow. We may not have toys right now, but we can plan how to build our snow castle and have lots of fun."

Jacey smiled. Great thinking, Zander.

"Yay." Caleb glanced over his shoulder at her and she nodded. He whipped back around to his new buddy. "What's a snow castle?"

"Come with me." Zander gently steered Caleb to the jacket he'd shed over an armchair. "I always carry paper and pen, so I'll draw you a picture and see if you like it."

Ah. She got it. He had it under control after all. He'd keep her son occupied, and happy. And soon they'd sit down to eat a meal. In the grand scheme of things, considering they survived unscratched from the accident, not counting a few bumps and bruises, there was a lot to be grateful for. When she and Caleb said their prayers later, she'd praise God left and right.

"But I need my toys for the castle," Caleb said, in full whine mode. "Mama only got one storybook from the car."

"It's snowing like crazy. Let's wait, partner."

Jacey remembered a plastic superhero of her son's still tucked in her purse. Maybe the trinket would pacify him. She excused herself to retrieve it from the bedroom. Once there, she grimaced at her reflection in the mirror. Her tangled mop of hair needed a good brushing. Not that she was straightening up to impress Zander. Definitely not.

The quiet jumped at her as she stepped out from the room. The two were gone.

Chapter 9

Jacey didn't waste time throwing a coat on. Evidently her son's episodes of fleeing outside when she wasn't looking weren't a thing of the past. And at his young age, anything could happen. She bolted to the door, flung it open, and ran out into the dark. Snow pelted her numb. It was late afternoon, but with the heavy storm clouds it could have been night.

"Caleb," she shouted.

No reply came from her son.

Nor from Zander.

Just as panic squeezed around her neck, Samson's bark ripped through the eerie silence. She headed toward the thicket of trees between the cabin and the Billings' house. Her jaw tightened. Had her son ran to the car? There were no approaching vehicle headlights brightening the otherwise dark and empty road. She breathed a little easier.

"Heigh-ho, heigh-ho, off to the cabin we go," came the singsong chant of Zander. Caleb echoed, the sweet sound cutting through the falling snow. Samson chimed in with a couple of woofs.

"Hey, guys," Jacey shouted. She shielded her eyes from the blowing snow. "Where are you?"

A gust of wind cracked, bending her over to dodge its ferocity.

"Jacey?"

"Mama?"

Jacey blinked several times and straightened. Zander stood before her with Caleb riding on his shoulders, his hands clamped tight around her son. Samson did guard duty beside them.

"I'm good. Just trying to escape this nasty wind." She rubbed her arms. Thank God Zander found her son within minutes. With the way her pumpkin could scamper off on the quick side, the possibilities of what might have happened if Zander didn't find Caleb as promptly as he did, and held onto him despite the wind, was too much to contemplate.

"Zander found me, Mama. And he picked me up."

"I see. Let's hurry to the cabin before we freeze like a snowman." She reached for Caleb. "Let's give your friend a break from holding you, my big boy."

Zander stepped sideways. "I got him. No problem."

"But what about your—"

"I have old horse hide. Tougher than I appear." He glanced at her son. "Your mama made a smart suggestion. It's time to be speedy, like we're jet planes."

"I'm a jet plane." Caleb extended his arms and made a zooming noise.

"Tower to plane, hear me buddy?"

"Yeah," came a high-pitched screech. "I hear ya."

"We're coming in for a landing. Prepare to enter cabin and eat ziti."

Caleb whooped and Samson yipped.

"Wait," Jacey called. "I'm a jet too." She spread her arms out as wings and made a buzzing sound.

Zander stamped his feet to shake off the snow. "What you are, Jacey, is pretty cool." He and her son flew off toward the cabin.

She rushed around the snow-covered picnic table and was about to dart indoors when an owl's hoot stopped her. She looked about, but didn't see the creature. With a deep breath she peered into the dark, almost night sky. She'd invite Zander to poke his head outdoors with her tomorrow evening, when the snow hopefully would have ended. They'd see a dusting of stars. Maybe hear more owls or the howling of coyotes. For now, she stepped into the warm, welcoming indoors of their temporary oasis. Once inside, she leaned against the shut door. Her eyes adjusted to the glowing yellow light, a grin on her son's face, and Zander's handsome features, the person, more and more, she didn't want to turn from.

THE FIRST SCREAM REACHED Jacey thick in a dream. She was sliding off the road into a snowbank and then saw robins perched on a tree newly budded with spring leaves. The second scream shot her upright in bed, the fantasy of sleep banished. Someone was hurt or in danger. She needed to get to that person and fast.

Nestled beside her in the double bed was Caleb, wearing one of Joe's borrowed flannel nightshirt tops. A little snore puffed from his lips. Sound asleep. Good. She slipped from the warmth of the down comforter. Cold quickly circled around her ankles despite the pair of wool socks, also a courtesy loan from Joe. She grabbed her sweater and draped it around the blue and white fleece top and jeans she'd fallen into bed with and padded to the door.

Snorts and moans came from the sofa where Zander camped out. She cracked the door open further. The oven light, left on in case of a night run to the bathroom, dimly reflected Samson's tail thumping wildly against the floor as he watched his master.

"Get down," Zander called. "You'll get hit." He thrashed his arms like he was trying to protect someone then covered his face, as if avoiding a direct blow to his head. "No . . . no, don't die."

Samson whimpered.

Jacey patted the collie's head. "Shh." She sat beside the tossing and turning man. "Zander," she said in a soft coo. "Wake up. You're having a—"

Oooof. He'd thrown his blanket over her head. Had she become part of his dream? Was he trying to protect her by hiding her from sight?

The dog barked.

Zander groped the sofa, eyes closed. "Samson?"

"He's fine."

Zander's brows crunched together. His lips parted slightly. "Jacey?"

"Over here." She covered him back up with the blanket. His bare arms poking out from a short-sleeved T-shirt were cold against her fingers. "Take it easy."

"What's happening?"

"You were having a nightmare."

"Did I hurt you?"

"No. Scared me, though."

He leaned back into his pillow and flung an arm across his eyes. "Don't write granny about this."

"Don't be embarrassed. We all have bad dreams."

"This wasn't a dream."

"Of course it was. You were asleep."

"More like my punishment."

"I don't understand."

He waved her off.

"No, you wait." Samson pressed against her. She was grateful for the dog's comforting presence. "You're upset. Don't go brushing me off. I want to help."

"Why? You have enough troubles to deal with."

"Label me different."

He shook. She pulled the blanket to his chin. Was this PTSD? She squeezed his hand. He didn't pull away.

"Zander, were you in combat? I'm a good listener if you need to talk."

He squeezed her hand back, their locked fingers warming. He yawned deeply and closed his eyes. "No military duty. It was . . ." A little snore escaped his lips.

Chapter 10

A soft tickle grazing his chin woke Zander. A wave of panic crashed through his chest when he couldn't move his legs. He tried again. Nothing.

He was paralyzed. Again.

God had forgotten about him. Again.

He peered down at his worthless lower body. Samson, stretched across his legs, shifted and pillowed his head on his knees. Ah. So, that was the source of his inability to move.

And his reason for giving up on God?

Nope. He wasn't going to go there. Not today. Probably not tomorrow or the next day either.

He glanced to his right and blinked when he saw Jacey on the floor slumped against the couch. Nope, not a dream but delicious reality. Eyes closed and her coat wrapped around her shoulders, she leaned toward him. Not a worry line was scrunched across her lovely face.

"Mama's sleeping," Caleb said softly.

Zander tilted his head and his ear crunched an object. He groped for the curiosity. A paper airplane? Probably explained the odd sensation on his chin. He looked at the boy seated at the table. "From you?" he mouthed.

Caleb scrambled over. "Want to play?" This time his tone leaned more toward rambunctious.

Zander lifted a finger toward his mouth and made a shushing noise.

Jacey stirred and cracked open one eye. "I'm awake. Talk away."

He smiled. How did someone who lost a place to live in as well as a job, get stuck in a blizzard and rely on the mercies of strangers, still manage to have a smile on her lips and look pretty, especially first thing in the morning? "Did you sleep there the whole night?"

She straightened, rubbing the arm she'd slept against. "Only after your nightmare set you screaming."

He wiggled free from Samson. His furry pal bounded off the couch, stretched and went straight to Caleb. The boy rewarded the dog with a big hug. Zander drew his knees to his chest and pressed his face onto his folded arms, his unshaved beard scraping his skin. Coiled muscles at the base of his neck burned. He mentally shrugged it away.

A soft touch came to his shoulder.

He glanced at Jacey.

"Last night, I was worried about you and didn't want to go back into the bedroom and leave you by yourself. Do you remember what happened?"

He shook his head, but then nodded. "Sort of." He screwed his eyes tight.

"Hey, it's okay."

"And how would you know?"

"No need to snap," she said softly.

He dropped his gaze. "You're right. I didn't sleep well. Nothing new, though." He looked back at her. Ruffled from sleep, part of her hair was puffed from frizz and the other half flattened straight. Lopsided and adorable. He mentally cursed himself for noticing.

She lifted her left hand and tapped it with her opposite thumb. "First," she ticked, "Your past isn't happening now."

She was right. Nothing from his past was presently occurring under the safety of this cabin's roof. He nodded.

She ticked the next finger. "Second, considering we wrecked our cars yesterday and could have been DOA ..." She peered over her shoulder at Caleb playing under the kitchen table with Samson. "We're pretty lucky. No, fortunate. Nah. Blessed."

He opened his mouth but she motioned for him to stop.

"Save the I-don't-believe-in-God spiel for another time."

"You're one determined lady."

"You bet I am."

He smiled. "I like that."

"You . . . wait . . . you like . . . what do you like?"

"Continue. You have me intrigued."

She flashed a wonky smile then raised her hands again. Her forehead wrinkled.

"You were at number three, Jacey."

She made a smacking noise with her lips. Part of him wanted to fantasize he'd heard a kiss rather than a note of frustration, but he fixed a straight face.

"Number three, it's daytime. Things are naturally better in the day."

"Better?" He craned his neck for a glance out of the picture window by the table. "This storm makes even morning look dark. I'm having doubts this snow will end soon."

She groaned. "Yes. Even if it's still snowing. Scary night monsters slink back into their caves or wherever they live during the day." She winked. "But have no fears, Z. I'll protect you."

"Z, huh?"

"And there's number four."

He lifted a brow.

"You heard me just fine. You're alive. We're alive. We get to begin over."

"And number five."

She shot to her feet. "I need to pee. You watch the troops and afterwards I'll muster breakfast." She trotted out of the room before he could reply.

It might have been only a few minutes—tops, seven—by the time Jacey entered the kitchen-dining area. The minty scent of toothpaste reached him before her smile. She'd brushed her hair and tied it back in a ponytail with one of those red fabric twisty things women use and had changed into a pullover sweater borrowed from Aubrey. The dark yellow complemented her golden hair. But, it didn't matter. Jacey would sparkle any time of day, regardless of what she wore or how she styled herself.

"There you are," he said, before the oven. "Don't worry about Caleb. Samson had to go out to do his, uh, morning business and Caleb promised to stay put. And Samson won't disappear, believe me. He wants his breakfast."

She stopped short, her sneakers squeaking on the tile flooring. "What are you doing?"

"Joe just dropped off breakfast. So, I'm holding an egg, watching a frying pan heat with a pat of butter spreading and talking with you."

"Ah. Thanks for the enlightenment."

"Hungry for scrambled eggs?"

She nodded then pointed at the tin percolator beginning to pop on a back burner. After sidestepping to his left side, she waved at the pot. "Hello, coffee, my friend. I doubted we would see each other for a few days."

"I can relate." He watched her set up two coffee mugs as he finished cracking the eggs into the pan and beat them with a fork. Considerate, for sure. She got his humor, which usually flew right over the heads of others. She was still comfortable with him, even after last night's theatrics. Just maybe something more could develop. No. Things like this didn't happen in real life. Not for him at least. He'd stick to the topic of food. "There's no milk for proper scrambled eggs, nor for the coffee. But I found four monster blueberry muffins in the bottomless bag Joe brought, along with three red apples. We have ourselves a bona fide feast, if you ask me. Besides, black coffee isn't awful."

In silence, she rushed to the window and slumped heavily against it as if she was pinned and couldn't get free.

"Hey, J, I promise my eggs will be edible and the coffee capable of opening the sleepiest of eyes. It's perc and not drip but . . ." Hmm. The way she averted eye contact with him stabbed at his worry button.

Her head drooped. A little whimper struggled free from her guarded lips.

He turned off the burner under the cooking eggs and hurried over. Without concern for proper etiquette nonsense or respect of overrated personal space, he touched her shoulder. "Forget this," he mumbled and fanned his fingers across her cheek. He wiped a couple of tears cascading down the small bruise from yesterday's accident, landing at the soft corner of her mouth. "Gotta level with you, Jacey." He lowered his tone to a murmur. "When I see a crying woman I want to do two things. I want to hug her silly until the sad leaves. Then, I want to punch the lights out of anyone who made her upset."

Slowly, Jacey faced him. A half sob, half chuckle escaped her sweet lips.

He raked his hand through his hair and groaned. "I've upset you more."

"No." She sniffled. "Just the opposite. You're the first adult in ages who has come along expressing genuine concern for me. I appreciate it."

"What's wrong with everyone? Look, I've known you for what? A day? And even I can see that you're a nice person, a caring soul, and an excellent, loving mom." He sighed exaggeratedly. "Despite you not liking my cooking."

She rubbed his arm. "Oh, stop."

"Let's have a seat and talk more." She opened her mouth but he hooked elbows and guided her over to the table and chairs. On the way, his hip froze and he stopped midstep.

"Zander?"

"If you're going to stick with me, at least for a while, get used to my body being uncooperative."

"The war?" She smacked her hands over her lips as soon as the word left her mouth.

"War?" He continued toward the table with her right beside him.

"Sorry. Just thinking about your dream last night."

He pulled out a chair. "Have a seat." He then sat besides her, sideways, and stared into the brightest, loveliest blue eyes he'd ever seen. "No war." The weight of what had happened six months ago was as awful as a war, and difficult to talk about. At the same time, he longed to share his story. Jacey wasn't any Plain Jane flitting temporarily in and out of his life.

Leave? He didn't want her to fly away after this snowstorm was over.

He squeezed his eyes shut.

Crazy. He must have gone mad, must have . . .

A hand pressed down on his.

"You spaced out on me."

His gaze dropped to their connected hands then lifted back to her pretty face. He sprang to his feet, stepped to the stove, and poured the dark roast brew into the two cups she'd set up. He brought the coffee over to the table.

She folded her hands around the mug, drew in a deep breath, and moaned in satisfaction. "A heap of thanks."

He took a swig of his own. "I wasn't in combat. Hope my screaming like a wimp last night didn't mislead you."

She tugged at his hand and smiled. "I prayed myself to sleep—beside you, by the sofa—asking God for the demons from your war memories to leave you in peace. But, I'm glad you weren't in a war. Although, I suspect that whatever situation you were in wasn't easy to take." She paused. "Am I putting it mildly?"

He nodded. "I am—was—am . . ." He licked his lips. "A police detective. In Baltimore. My partner, Chloe, and I were on the way back after conducting a few street interviews on this crack house undergoing surveillance. It was late and we'd stopped for a cup of coffee at a convenience store. Chloe insisted she go in and I wait in the car. We were in our street clothes, driving my car." He snaked his hand free of hers. His hand immediately turned cold, as if plunged into a bucket of ice. He rubbed his face.

"If it's too much to share, you don't have to." She reached out again and touched his arm. "My tiny shoulders are yours to lean on, though."

He dragged his hands down his face and stopped at his jaw. "You're amazing."

She made air quotes with her fingers. "As in 'amazing' like I have some nerve or 'amazing' like—"

He seized her hands and cradled them midair within his own as if grasping a fragile bird. "Amazing, as in sweet. As in, I'm a lucky guy to have you listening to me."

Red crept up her cheeks. "Not the amazing, as in I'm the person who smashed into your car and nearly killed us both?"

He shrugged. "Yeah. That too." He lowered their coupled hands to the table where they remained united. "Chloe was taking a while. I didn't like it and went in. The second I entered the store, a punk kid shot the wrong-place, wrong-time clerk working the register. Chloe was flopped over the counter. I didn't know it at the time, but she was bleeding out from a knife wound. The perp saw me and shot off a round with Chloe's pistol. I managed to fire back before I passed out from his hit. I woke up in the hospital." He blinked away the visual of a dying Chloe and focused on Jacey. A very alive, wonderful Jacey. "In my dream, uh . . . it might be me trying to save her instead of, in reality, being seconds too late."

Her throat convulsed a few times. "What a tragedy. For you and your partner. It's a shame the poor kid got to that awful place in life to begin with. Did he die?"

He stared at the far corner of the table. "Yes. The kid died from my bullet. Immediately. And I'm not sorry. Chloe was a new mom—her baby only seven months old." He slowly faced her. "Not what you wanted to hear, huh?"

"It was an unfortunate circumstance. I'm not going to judge you. It's not my place."

"Whose place is it? Your loving God's?"

She crossed her arms, yet didn't look away. "God loves you, your partner, and the punk kid."

"His name was Kyle," he said through a tight voice. "He was sixteen, homeless, and living with gang members. Hungry and wanting a smoke, he held up the store. His first gamble with crime, and his last."

"Wow. I can understand why you'd have nightmares over it."

"Plural? How do you know it wasn't a one-time embarrassing dream last night?"

She leaned over the table. "I don't. But I know one thing. If it were me, Z, I'd be having nightmare after nightmare over those lost lives." She inched closer to his face. "And I'd feel guilty, too."

His neck tightened. "Over shooting Kyle?"

"No. You needed to defend yourself. The guilty part is over giving up on God, thinking He hates you for protecting yourself." She ran her fingertips along the table's edge. "Getting back to what happened—this explains your injury and subsequent pain, and your confusion as to whether you're on the force or not?"

He nodded. "You're good at figuring things out."

"How bad were you hurt?"

"My lower back had substantial nerve damage that impacted my hip and leg. Missed my spine, though. Temporary paralysis. Spent time in rehab. Afterward I couldn't live on my own and moved in with my cousin. With him getting married in a couple of months it was time for me to become independent again. I'm on the way north to stay at one of my folks' apartments until I can manage to get my act together and figure out the next move in life."

She dragged a short-trimmed fingernail across the table's surface. "Sounds like we're both on the way to the next chapter in our lives." She huffed from the corner of her mouth. "Even if we don't know where we're heading to."

He leaned back and studied her. A smile came easily to his lips then, considering he'd disclosed seconds ago the turmoil he'd spent what had felt like an eternity keeping hidden from others.

"What are you thinking?" she squeaked.

"I hate talking about myself, but you did an excellent job getting that stuff out of me."

"I care about you."

He pulled at his chin, trying to wrap his mind around those words. Warmth zinged him silly. "Now, tell me the truth. A few minutes ago, was it the visual of me standing before the stove cooking you breakfast that sent you hightailing from me?"

"Not at all." She sat straighter. "You reminded me of the diner where I worked for the past three years, and kinda like my mother."

"Hmm. Not sure I want to hear about how I could remind you of your mom."

"Really? My mom was a saint."

"Then, I'm no competition for her." Unsure whether the caffeine or Jacey's undivided attention caused his happy buzz, he guzzled the rest of his coffee.

She inhaled deeply, her small shoulders squaring back on her petite frame. "I'm in need of finding a new home, and with a four-year-old in tow, mind you, I'm a bit shaken. It's not easy raising a little boy myself."

"No husband?" He cringed. "Oops. Not my business."

"I don't mind sharing. Josh and I were married, but when he found out I was pregnant with Caleb he took off. Filed for divorce. End of nasty story."

"Sorry to hear that." Zander shoved the coffee mug aside and reached for her hand. "So, you had Caleb at age nineteen . . . twenty-two?"

"Josh and I were married after college graduation. Caleb came along when I was about to turn twenty-five."

He mentally did the math. "You don't look like you're about to turn thirty, not that thirty's old."

"Good. There are days I feel way older."

"If you're curious, I'm thirty-four."

"Well, yeah, I was curious. Just wanted to mind my biz."

He smiled. "Are you always good and polite?"

"Someone has to be."

He wagged a finger at her.

"But, like you, I'm moving on."

He nodded. "I'm heading north and you south."

"And our paths crossed in the extreme."

"All right. I give up. How do I remind you of your mom? I can't imagine."

"When I saw you at the stove, a memory of her making me breakfast flickered before my eyes. My stepdad's a whole different story, but Mom was a lovely person. A great mother. And at times, my best friend." She sniffled. "I miss her. She passed a year ago. Having to take care of her, she was another reason why I called out of work as often as I did."

"I'm close to my mom and can't imagine losing her." He offered a little grin. "But Jacey, this is why my cooking shouldn't make you weepy." He ticked his thumb. "First, I'm not your boss and definitely am not your mom. And as far as that boss of yours goes, it's a good thing for his sake he's not here with us right now." He winked. "Believe me, he hasn't messed with anyone like me before, disabled or not."

She gave him a slow perusal. "You're quite able-bodied."

Heat crept up his neck but he wasn't going to go there. He ticked his opposite index finger. "I can't understand husbands or significant others who leave their woman when a child's on the way. Not cool. While we're here, I'll keep a protective watch over you and Caleb. No worries."

Caleb.

She gasped. "It's too quiet out there," she said over her shoulder as she rushed to the door.

He followed. "I'm right beside you."

Chapter 11

Outside of the warm cabin, Jacey cupped her hands megaphone style, and shouted Caleb's name. Each breath clouded the cold air. The whipping of the wind was the only response. It was downright miserable with the snow pelting down as if it were trying to make a mark in the history books as the worst storm of the century. Her poor little boy would freeze. She forced back the edgy panic building in her chest away. *Father, please help me find my son.*

A touch came to her shoulder. She turned slightly. Zander stood inches from her, silhouetted against a row of white frosted fir trees.

"Do you see him?" She clung to hope.

He shook his head. "Not yet, but we'll find him. Don't worry." His mouth grew tight. "This is all my fault. I shouldn't have let a four-year-old outdoors with an energetic dog. What was I thinking? With my past history—"

She reached for his arms. "This is my fault too." The time chatting with Zander back in the cabin might have equaled the cozy comfort of meeting up with an old pal, but her sweet pumpkin loved to explore, and moved about fast. She should have made sure he was indoors within two minutes tops. "Let's not spend the time in anger or regret. Got that?"

"Okay," he said softly. He slipped his jacket over her shoulders. "You're not getting frostbitten on my watch."

She pulled the garment tight around her, and recalled how he looked after her right after the crash when he'd also insisted she keep warm by offering his jacket. "But I have my coat. What about you?"

"Then keep doubly warm. I'm fine."

"Yeah, right."

"Determination to find Caleb is fueling me plenty. Listen, I'll go right. You left."

Before she could say more, Zander ducked around the corner of the cabin, shouting Caleb and Samson's names.

Jacey zoomed left, also shouting their names until the raw cold froze her voice. When she reached the steep hillside, she mustered another shout. The wind carried back a dog's bark.

Out of the corner of her eye she saw Zander moving away from the hill. She called out to him and waved frantically with both arms. A blast of cold hit her, robbing her of breath and she pressed her hands against her chest.

"Jacey?"

She blinked. He'd rushed to her side so fast. "Yeah . . . just . . . winded."

He wrapped an arm around her shoulders and pulled her tight against him, enveloping her with warmth as if he'd covered them both with a heated blanket. "See Caleb?"

She shook her head. "I think I heard Samson." She pointed at the hill.

Zander backed away from her a few inches and whistled three times.

A woof came from a distance.

Zander whistled again.

A whooshing noise funneled its way down the hillside. Seconds later the black-and-white blur of Samson barreled toward them.

"Good boy," Zander said when Samson reached his side. The dog leaned against his leg and barked. Zander peered up the hill. "Caleb's got to be up there."

He patted the dog's side. "Find Caleb. Go, boy."

The dog rushed back up the hill.

"Ready?" he asked.

"Nothing's keeping me from Caleb, but what about you? Can you manage the hill?"

"Nothing's keeping me from Caleb," Zander echoed Jacey's words. He hooked arms with her. "*Nothing.*"

The climb was similar to when she and Zander first walked toward the Billings' house. A few steps forward, she'd slip and he would catch her. Then it would be his turn and she'd grabbed his arm to help steady him. Again, side-by-side, they took each step together.

Midway up, Jacey pointed toward the hill's peak. "You think Samson's right?"

"He's pure Border collie. Centuries of herding animals are inbred in him. He's bringing us toward Caleb."

She pressed a finger against her mouth, trying to stop her trembling lips.

He squeezed her hand. "We'll find him."

"But what happens if—"

"Don't think it. Don't visualize it. He will be fine."

Zander was right. Focus on God and pray for His mercies on her son.

They finally crested the hill and paused, catching their breath while Samson bounded around them. Stretching ahead was a flat area covered in deepening snow, and beyond that dense woods swallowed the openness. Jacey rubbed her arms. Caleb could have run into the woods in search of another adventure like she'd promised him yesterday. She scanned their surroundings, but there was no sign of her little boy, like footsteps, though the fresh snow probably was covering them.

Samson dodged across the field to the right. He stopped in the distance.

Zander strode two steps then slipped. A long *aaahh* escaped his lips.

Jacey dropped to his side. She didn't like the looks of his furrowed brow and squinty eyes. "You okay?"

"You bet."

She extended a hand. "Here. I'll help you up."

He stood on his own and brushed the snow from his clothes. "Embarrassed, that's all."

"More like strong willed." She mustered a small grin. "That's a good thing."

"As long as you think so."

She did, but she'd reply back to him later, when they were all snuggled down in the warm cabin again. "What's Samson standing next to?"

"Looks like a fallen tree."

"Oh . . . my . . ."

"Hold tight, Jacey. Let's go see. Don't let fear rob your energy."

"Easy for you to say," she mumbled. As soon as the words flew from her mouth, regret stabbed her tongue.

Zander seized her hand again. "I get fear. And get how you're afraid of the worst right now. Don't blame you. But Jacey, though I'm sure Caleb is okay, he's going to need our strength to help him off this hill and back down to the cabin's safety."

She slowly nodded. He was right. But. And there were many *buts*. Countless things could be wrong. Her heart pounded in her ears. If she lost Caleb, she'd lose her reason to live.

"Jacey," Zander called.

He pulled her from the anguish dragging her down and she glanced over.

"You believe in God?"

"Yes."

"Then show me."

She blinked. "I don't understand."

"Show me how you cling to the God you believe won't fail you."

For a man seemingly inclined to hide his heart from a Father he questioned, Zander was one hundred percent right. She did believe in God. And this wasn't the time to doubt Him.

She nodded. "I believe in God. I trust Him and believe He will bring us to a safe and healthy Caleb."

"That's my Jacey."

His Jacey? She tightened her grip on his hand and led him, inch by snowy inch, toward the downed tree.

Chapter 12

Jacey reached the small white pine tree first. "Calm down, buddy," she said to Samson. The Border collie kept to his own agenda and continued barking.

"Good boy," Zander said when he reached Jacey a moment afterward. When the dog woofed again, Zander commanded him to be quiet.

A faint sound reached Jacey's ears. "Mama."

She fell to her knees. "Caleb, are you under the tree? Are you hurt, baby?"

"No hurt, Mama. I made a tunnel under the tree, but I got stuck."

She used her bare hands to frantically brush snow away from the tree. Within seconds, she reached the tunnel and smiled. "There you are. Wait a second. Are you a snowman or my son?"

"I'm Caleb, Mama."

"You are, you are. Hang on. We're going to get you out."

Zander sank to the ground beside her. "Did the tree fall on top of you, Caleb?"

"No. Samson and me took a walk. He wanted to play and I saw this tree and found this hole. We made a secret tunnel and . . ." He began to whimper.

Jacey touched his cheek. "Honey, don't be afraid. We'll help you."

"How are you stuck?" Zander asked.

"My boot."

Jacey shuddered. Her baby couldn't move. Probably freezing . . . on the verge of hypothermia? A scream rushed to her lips. No, don't yell. Don't let Caleb hear how upset you are. Stay strong for him. "Does your foot or legs hurt?"

"No, Mama. I just can't move my foot. And I'm cold."

"I'm going to get you loose real fast, Caleb, and get you warm." Zander said. "I want you to be a big, brave boy for both your mama and me. Okay?"

"Uh-huh."

"That's my boy." He patted Jacey's shoulder. "I'm going to look for a branch to pry up this tree. Fortunately it's a young one and isn't too big. Looks like the hole he's in isn't filled with snow. That gives us a bit of leeway to work with."

"What about your back?"

"I'll do whatever it takes to get Caleb free and back to the cabin safe and sound. Besides, I have a huge incentive."

She rubbed her hands together and blew on them. "What's that, Z?"

"I want to see the two of you cuddled and falling asleep with smiles on your faces."

Gratitude sailed from her heart to her lips. "Thank you."

Zander grunted and pushed to his feet, commanded Samson to stay, and then headed toward the woods.

She watched him dash through the snow at a quick pace despite the awkward way his hips and legs moved. He was ignoring his pain to help her son. She clutched her icy fingers around his jacket—the one he urged her to wear—and tugged it tighter and sniffled.

"Mama," Caleb called. "I'm being a big boy."

She turned back to the fallen tree and her heart fluttered in relief over the strength in her son's voice. "You are, sweetheart. I'm so proud of you."

"But I'm cold."

"Zander is coming back right now," she said. "Wow. Wait until you see the size of the branches he found to move this tree trunk off of you." For a man recently badly injured, he was pretty jaw-dropping wonderful. Hmm. Throw in downright handsome . . . in both the looks and the compassion departments.

Samson let loose a happy bark and circled his master.

Zander wedged the larger branch under the trunk. "Mama," he said to Jacey, "why don't you and Samson hold Caleb's hand?"

"Zander?" Caleb called.

"Yes?"

"Dogs don't have hands."

Zander flashed a grin at Jacey. "Your son's amazing," he murmured. "Like you."

Warmth flooded her from head to toe. He'd chased away the numbing cold from deep within her. "Thank you," she mouthed, too breathless to speak.

He knelt and stuck his face into the cavity under the tree then instructed Caleb to say *shake hands* to Samson. When her son did, the dog extended a front paw toward him. Zander got to his feet.

"What's the game plan, Z?"

He scooped up the second, smaller branch and handed it to her. "This is for extra protection. On a count of three I'm going to put my weight down on the big limb. It should lift the tree just enough for you to slide the smaller branch under for added support. Then I want you to scoot under, free Caleb's foot, and pull him to safety. If need be, wiggle his foot loose from the boot."

"Got it."

Zander counted to three then huffed and heaved. The tree cleared just enough for her to work. A rock wedged tight against her son's right boot. After a few attempts, she managed to unsnap his boot and shimmy his foot free.

"I got him," she yelled. Jacey pulled Caleb, scooped him up for what she planned to be a lifetime embrace then slid Zander's jacket from her shoulders and wrapped Caleb in it. "You're okay, baby. I love you, honey."

Zander lowered the tree and hugged the two tight.

Caleb darted his gaze from Jacey to Zander then back to Jacey and frowned. "Are you and Zander mad at me? Or Samson?"

She stroked his cheek. "No way."

"They why you're crying, Mama?"

She sniffled. "Because I'm happy."

"You're silly, Mama."

"Caleb," Zander said. "Your mama is pretty awesome."

"That's because she's my mama."

Zander hooked arms with her and together they followed Samson down the hillside.

When they reached the bottom Caleb poked his arm out from Jacey's protective hold. "Look. It stopped snowing."

"Yay," Jacey and Zander said together. Big smiles crept across their faces.

She patted her son's head. "We'll have a happily ever after ending, after all. Just like in your storybooks."

Caleb beamed. "I like happy stories."

Zander flashed her a sly grin.

"What's the face for, Z?"

He crossed his arms. "We'll definitely have a happy finish. Know why?"

"Why?" Caleb shouted, answering for her.

Jacey giggled, a reaction she couldn't have predicted. "Why?" she said, matching her son's enthusiasm and volume.

"Because we'll make it wonderful. Nothing, including a blizzard, will stop us."

Chapter 13

Zander expected to pay a price for hauling the branch and then lifting the tree trunk off Caleb, but the fire now spreading through his body was crazy. His appetite gone, he stared at his sandwich of turkey and Swiss cheese. At this point, he'd be willing to forfeit vacations plus listening to classical music in exchange for a painkiller.

"Need more mayo?" Jacey asked from her seat beside him at the table.

Caustic barbs pocked his tongue and threatened to shove him down a turbulent river. He swallowed his crankiness back. "I'm not fussy."

She glanced at his mostly untouched lunch. "You certainly earned a hearty appetite rescuing Caleb out in the tundra."

He shrugged. "At least it stopped snowing."

"Mama, someone is coming," Caleb said in front of the window where he and Samson were playing.

"Is it Joe?"

"Nope. A woman."

Zander couldn't guess who'd be coming over, but he welcomed the interruption. Up to minutes ago, Jacey's heart was full with worry over her son. He didn't need to heap his own problems on her too.

Caleb zipped to the door and yanked it open. Cold stampeded in, along with a cheery hello.

A woman, pale but with a lovely smile, stooped to the boy's height. "You must be Caleb. I'm Aubrey, Joe's wife."

"Uh-huh. I'm Caleb." He pointed to his feet. "I got stuck in the snow and Zander got me unstuck and now I have only one shoe."

"I'll look around and see if I can find my grandson's extra set. He's just your size."

Jacey rushed to her son's side and placed her hands on his shoulders. "It's nice to finally meet you, Aubrey. Come on in and I'll close the door to the winter's cold."

The woman stomped the snow from her boots. "At least it's clearing up outside."

"That certainly is great news." Jacey gestured to her son and then Zander. "Thank you for lending us your cabin. I don't know what we would have done without your and Joe's kindness. And also thanks for all the delicious food your husband's brought over . . . and possibly extra shoes for my son."

Zander pushed onto his feet. "Yes, we both appreciate your consideration. How are you? Joe told us you've had the flu."

Aubrey slid off her gray woolen coat and matching hat to reveal a bright red-and-white holiday sweater of Santa and his reindeer riding the night sky. Her green slacks added to the festive mood. Christmas. He'd hoped to be opening gifts with his folks and enjoying the holiday brunch his mom always cooked. Now the presents were smashed in his wrecked car. He rubbed his neck, while glancing at Jacey. Then again, he never would have imagined meeting this beautiful woman and her adorable son.

"Offering you the cabin is the least we can do. Thank God the three of you weren't hurt in that awful car accident." Aubrey nodded at Zander. "I've been ill but I'm better, thanks. Bad timing, with Christmas three days from today. I have tons of holiday preparation to get the house ready for our grandkids. That is, if they and my daughter and son-in-law can fly in from Colorado. They're also having a doozy of a storm." She pulled out a paper bag from her coat pocket. "Like oranges?"

Caleb bounced on his toes. "I love oranges. They're peely. But where's Joe?"

Aubrey handed the fruit to the boy and watched him carry it to the table. "I'm afraid Joe's now the one sick in bed with the flu."

"Oh, I'm sorry," Zander said as he moved beside Jacey. Funny, as soon as he got closer to her his pain abated a notch. "What can we do?"

"Well . . ."

"Tell us," Jacey said.

Aubrey nodded. "Joe hoped to clear the snow from the walk, the trail to the woodpile, and make a path between the house and the cabin. And the driveway, although that could wait until the town sends out the plows to clear the roads since no one is going anywhere until then."

Jacey inched even closer to Zander. "Do you have a snow blower?"

"It quit working end of last winter. I told Joe to get it fixed or replace it, but he was in denial that autumn was going to turn into Old Man Winter."

"A shovel?" Zander asked.

Aubrey's hazel eyes brightened. "We definitely have a couple of those."

"ZANDER," JACEY CALLED from the cabin's door as he marched toward Joe and Aubrey's barn. Samson trailed him. "You wonderful but stubborn man," she muttered under her breath as she closed the door.

"Mama, why's Zander stubborn?"

She grimaced. Apparently, she didn't mumble soft enough. "Would you like to go outside and watch me and Zander shovel snow for Aubrey and Joe?"

Caleb glanced at his new, borrowed boots, courtesy of Aubrey's absent grandson. "Can I play with Samson?"

"Absolutely, sweetheart. But you must promise to stay close by and not wander off."

"Okay. No more trees." He struggled into his jacket. "But why's Zander stubborn?"

She should have known he wouldn't forget his question. He never did. "I meant to say Zander is determined."

"Is that good?"

She held back a sigh. Yes. His tenacity helped him persevere during his recovery from his gunshot wound. No. Stubbornness could cause him to overdo it physically. She'd caught him flinching and holding his breath a few times since they'd come down from the hill to the cabin after finding Caleb. She needed to help him, but how could she explain all this to her four-year-old son?

She fastened Caleb's coat hood. "Determination is good to have. It helps you to do more than you think you can." She tapped her chin twice. "Remember the last time, like Joe, when you were sick in bed with a nasty cold?"

"Uh-huh. I didn't want to play."

"Correct. But you listened to what I said. You rested, drank and ate, and stayed in bed. Remember why?"

"If I rested, I'd get better faster."

She smiled. "What a great memory you have! You were determined to get well, and you did."

Caleb pulled his bottom lip. "Is Zander sick with a cold? I like him, Mama. I don't want him sick."

"Zander's fine." And with her help, hopefully he won't be in worse shape.

I like him, Mama.

Her heart skipped a beat.

She liked Zander too. A lot.

SAMSON BARKED, STOOD on his hind legs, and planted his frosty paws on Zander's waist.

"Yeah, I see them, buddy." He watched as Jacey and Caleb clumped their way over. Their pink and blue coats were bright against the white snow and mottled purple and gray sky.

Samson trotted off to the woman and child.

"Sure, change loyalty on me." His gaze shifted from the cute, laughing boy to his attractive mom. "Don't blame you one bit."

"Hey, Z."

There she was, straight out of his daydreams. Shiny blonde hair. Bluest of blue eyes. And a smile that nearly arrested his heart every time he saw her.

She waved a shovel at him.

"Oh, no you're not."

Her smiled tightened. "Oh, yes I am going to help. I shovel snow all the time."

He scooped a heaping shovelful of snow. No way would he let her work her bones off while he was perfectly capable. "This stuff may be the light, snowball-making kind, but I can't let you help dig us out."

Her smile flattened into a grin. "You know, I'm not asking your permission. Besides, it's you I'm worried about."

"Oh, I'm no concern."

She shook a finger at him. "You are too."

He glanced over his shoulder. "What about Caleb?"

"I've talked to him about staying in my sight. Besides, shoveling is good exercise. Keeps me in shape during the winter months."

"You're already in good shape," he murmured.

"Pardon?"

Amused, he shook his head. He could tell by the rosy hue spreading across her cheeks she'd heard exactly what he'd said.

He scooped another load of snow. "Suit yourself."

She gave him a quick perusal from head to toe. "I believe I will."

Aware he was at her delightful mercy and not the other way around, he gulped. A tiny part of him wanted to order her back into the cabin.

She shouldn't be outdoors in this cold weather. He wanted to protect her, to coddle her. When he was with her he felt . . . what? Appreciated? Yep. Happy? Definitely. Loved? He smiled to himself. Yeah, loved. He hadn't felt this good, at least mentally, since before the shooting. Yet, with each second he spent with Jacey, the past faded fast. Now was all that counted. He wanted her beside him.

"Okay, then. But if we have to be outdoors in this stinking cold, let's have a bit of fun."

He moved closer by a foot. She took a step toward him. They continued to narrow the distance between them until a mere couple of inches remained.

With a sharp breath the scent of the pine scented cabin, cocoa, and her coconut shampoo, wafted upward. Every muscle in him uncoiled.

"What's your version of fun, Z?"

"You just had to ask, huh?" He flung the snow at her and darted off toward the road.

"No way," she shouted. "Prepare for revenge."

A quick glance over his shoulder showed her prancing through the snow after him, her shovel poised in the air like a weapon. Caleb, keeping his promise to his mama, followed. Samson leapt in the snow after the boy.

Zander slowed down, wanting all of them to catch up with him.

Chapter 14

If it weren't for Caleb's potty needs and wanting hot chocolate, Jacey had no qualms about remaining outdoors with the man she found fascinating, fun, and fabulously attractive. In her book, those three Fs equaled an A-plus. A cloud of mystery shadowed him, but she wanted to know everything about Zander . . . if it was meant to be. Her fluttery, erratic heartbeat every time their eyes met hinted that might indeed be the case.

"Is the cocoa ready?" Caleb asked.

"Yes, sweetie." She poured the water into the mug and stirred well before placing it before her son along with the reminder to blow on it.

Samson, sticking to the boy's side like peanut butter to bread, woofed.

"Mama, Samson's hungry too. Can he have cocoa?"

"Dogs can't have cocoa, but Zander will give him a doggie biscuit for a snack. After the shoveling, we all deserve a goody."

Her treat would be chatting with him. His presence would be all the sugar she'd need to make her afternoon delightful. She moved to the window to watch for his return.

As if on cue, the cabin's door opened and the man in her thoughts strode in. Samson barked and Caleb squealed. The sounds of a home. Jacey smiled, loving every second.

He pushed the door shut then leaned against it. And froze in place.

Jacey rushed over. "You're pale, clenching your fists, and your forehead's wrinkled. What's wrong?"

His frown deepened. "Nice compliment."

"And you're sarcastic, which you don't do."

"How do you know? We've only known each other—"

She rubbed his arm. "I know enough about you to know a tease from a bite to a cry for help."

He averted his eyes.

She fanned her fingers across his cheek, hearing a slight hitch in his breath. She leaned closer to keep her words from reaching Caleb's ears and stood on her toes to whisper into his ear. She lost her balance and her mouth swept close to his lips.

She couldn't turn away from him.

He didn't try.

"And I know you well enough," he said in a hushed tone, "to know that wasn't intentional."

"Sorry."

"Don't be. I liked it."

"You're in pain, Z."

"Guess you *do* know me."

She nodded. "Let me help you to the sofa."

He slipped his arm around her middle and tightened his grasp. "Slowly. I don't want to worry Caleb."

"Yep, cowboy." He couldn't pull the let's-not-worry-your-son bit with her. His pain was getting out of control, forcing him to move much slower than his normal pace. "Caleb," she said, "why don't you play with Samson in the bedroom?" Her pumpkin raced out of sight, calling the dog's name and giggling.

She helped Zander stretch across the two sofa cushions and positioned the end pillow to support his head. He puffed out a few grunts as she hovered over him. Not good at all.

She jutted her chin toward his duffel bag parked alongside the end table. "Got any pain pills in there?"

"Ibuprofen."

"That's it?"

He squeezed his eyes shut for a span of seconds then opened them. "I took myself off the heavier stuff. Didn't want to get addicted."

"Probably smart, but pain's not fun. Just hope the ibuprofen is strong enough this time." She stood. "Let me get you some water and forage for crackers or something to stave off stomach upset and then I'll slip you a couple of pills."

"Make it three."

On a makeshift tray of a dinner plate, she brought him over a glass of water, a dry slice of wheat bread, and sat beside him. He didn't inch away. Their bodies pressed tight against each other. Rather than focusing on the provisions she offered, she caught him staring at the place where her hip touched his side. The warm spot they shared.

"Can you sit upright to take this?"

He shook his head. "I think I'm stuck."

After setting the plate down on the floor, she slipped her arm under his upper back and slowly helped him sit up. She didn't want to move her hands away, but had no choice. "Here you go," she said, handing him the glass and ibuprofen.

After gulping down the pills and swigging the water, he took the bread and bit off a small corner. Two handfuls of seconds passed and then he chewed off another piece of bread. He needed more sustenance after that hard outdoor work. If anything, he needed to counter the side effects of the pills. "Is the pain interfering with eating?"

He crumpled the bread in his fist. "Let's just say that sleep may be the best solution."

On her feet again, she called out to Caleb. "Sweetheart, I'll be right back. Be on the quiet side so Zander could rest."

"Where're you going?" Zander asked, his eyes already shut.

"I'm making a quick dart down to the main house to see if Aubrey has a heating pad we can borrow. Between the ibuprofen and heat, your muscles should calm down a bit. Then, I'll show you my next plan."

"Which is?"

"You rest, Z. I'll show you later."

AUBREY'S JOY AND THANKFULNESS over having the walk and driveway shoveled quickly turned to worry as Jacey told her about Zander's pain. The older woman piled Jacey's arms with not only a heating pad, but also a batch of homemade chicken dumpling soup and a loaded plastic container of freshly baked cornbread.

"Since I'm back on my feet, I'm cooking and baking to compensate for lost time. This soup is one of Joe's favorites." Aubrey opened the door for her. "I need to check on Joe. You go watch over your two men."

Jacey held back a chuckle. "Caleb is all the man I need in my life."

Aubrey patted Jacey's arms. "Sweetie, Zander's a good person. Believe me, I can tell. And good souls are hard to find. He's a keeper."

Jacey's history gave plenty of testimony as to how hard it was to find good souls, and although she was attracted to Zander . . .

Attracted.

Ah, attracted. A delightful rippling spread inside of her whenever she saw Zander. When apart, he shimmered like sparklers through her mind. But was this giddy emotion more than attraction? Loving another person meant trusting them, but loved ones could give into betrayal, such as was the case with both her stepdad and husband.

She lifted the bundle of supplies in her hand. "You and Joe have been most kind. We can never thank you enough. Please tell your husband I hope he makes a fast recovery." With that, she was on her way back to the cabin.

Back to her little boy.

And back to her man?

JACEY EASED OPEN THE cabin door. Caleb and Zander were snuggled together on the couch under the blanket. Zander held the one storybook they'd managed to extract from the car while Caleb pointed at a page and pretended to read it aloud. Samson sat on the floor, his furry head draped across her son's lap. If only she had her cell phone. What a picture she could take, one that she'd treasure for years. Instead, the device was stuck in the car, packed in a tote rather than her purse.

"Don't you two look cozy?" To her own ears she sounded happy, and it felt good. Aubrey was right. Jacey needed to be back with *her men* to watch over them.

"Mama, you're home."

Had Zander, whose eyes were now heavy-hooded with drowsiness, caught Caleb's word choice of *home*?

Her son glanced at Zander then back to her. "Can you snuggle with us?"

"I'd like to, pumpkin, but come help me first."

Five minutes later, with the soup warming on low and Caleb and Samson playing fort under the kitchen table, she sat beside Zander.

He opened his eyes. "So, will you cuddle with me?"

She grinned. "Oh, so you did hear Caleb. You looked like you were drifting off to sleep. They say cuddling is good for the soul." She slipped the heating pad under his back. "First things first. Relax with this heat. It will ease your aches. We'll be eating lunch soon."

He grasped her hands and gave a gentle squeeze. "I'm already feeling better and it's not the ibuprofen or the heat."

"Do you say that to all the women who bring you heating pads and the promise of lunch?"

His fingers trailed up her arm and then leapt to her face. He caressed her cheek. "I'm not sure I've ever said that to anyone."

She turned away.

"Don't," he murmured. "I like looking at you."

She stood.

"Jacey?"

She held up an index finger and moved to the kitchen. Quickly, she turned off the warming soup. Lunch could wait and Caleb needed a nap. She glanced under the table and discovered both boy and dog curled together snoozing. Perfect. She returned to Zander and switched off the heating pad. "Turn over."

His eyes widened.

"Trust me, Z?"

"Absolutely."

She helped him onto his stomach and began massaging his back, rejoicing in his pleasurable sighs.

"You're a masseuse too?"

"Nah. I just know what feels good on my own body." She covered her mouth.

"I might not be able to see you this second," he said into the sofa's cushion, "but I bet your cheeks are coloring apple red." He grunted when she hit a tight muscle. "I give you lots of credit for waiting on customers all day. I couldn't do it. One gripe from them and I'd give it right back to them."

"A living is a living. For the most part, people are interesting and kind." Her hands stopped at the last word. "Did you always want to become a detective?"

"Changing topics on me?"

"You noticed."

He chuckled, a pleasant tune to her ears.

"You're sounding better."

He turned onto his side toward her without a trace of pain. "I am, and it's because of you."

She traced her finger along his bottom lip. "How do you know it's not from God answering my prayers over you?"

He nodded. "Might be both. I've been doing a little praying myself since we've become stranded together. Been asking God why He semi-marooned me with this beautiful woman. Been telling Him I can't guess what's ahead of me, but I'm figuring since He's saved my life twice, first from the bullet and then from what could have been a much worse car accident, He must have a hefty amount of good in mind."

Jacey swiped at her eyes. "Answer my question before I blubber like a baby."

"Over becoming a detective?"

She nodded.

He kept silent a moment. "Yep. After watching crime series on TV and reading mystery novels throughout junior and senior high, I wanted to become a detective. And you?"

She snuck a hand behind him and began to rub his back again lightly. He pretended to purr like a cat. She liked she could do that little for him.

"I met and fell in love with Caleb's dad, Josh, right after I began my junior year in college. He promised me the sun and moon and I leapt into the horizon with him."

"Poetic."

She sighed. "I was a literature major. Might have taught it or gone into writing, but instead we married right after school. Life with Josh slid from Disney wonderful to hanging in there to why-did-I-marry-him seemingly overnight. And as I'd shared, when I learned I was pregnant with Caleb, Josh took off for better places and sent me the divorce papers. He has nothing to do with his son."

Zander mumbled a curse. "The jerk. I've known you for far less time and already know the better place is with you. And Caleb."

"You're kind." She glanced at her son under the table, grateful for the sense of privacy her sleeping son, alongside Samson, gave her.

Zander touched her cheek. With the tips of his fingers he brought her lips to his own waiting mouth.

She tasted strength, assurance, and all that was fiercely masculine. She tasted a sliver of tomorrow, of hope. Of goodness.

She wasn't sure who pulled back first, or when, but they smiled widely at each other.

"I could get used to this," he said. "A cozy home with you and Caleb."

"And Samson."

"A whole herd of dogs. Cats too." He peered into her eyes. "And others."

She nodded, staring at the twinkle in his eyes. Did he mean other types of pets . . . or children? A tingle crawled up her arm. Could she dare to dream?

He scooted tight against the sofa's back and patted the bare spot between them. She swung her feet onto the sofa and snuggled beside him, above the blanket, with their backs against the throw pillows. No rushing into things like she once carelessly did with Josh.

"Tell me something I don't know about you, Z."

"Like what?"

"Well, what kind of music do you like?"

He scrubbed his face with his hands. "If I tell you, you'll run for the proverbial hills."

She lifted a brow. "Why? You're into grunge rock?"

"Classical. Love my Bach, Beethoven, and Chopin."

"And you think I'm a classical snob?"

"I'm used to women frowning when they hear my taste of music. And you?"

"Well, I did take violin lessons for two years." A charming smile lit his face, reminding her of a streak of sunshine between storm clouds. "Then I tried folk guitar. These days it's whatever's on the radio or Caleb's children's songs."

"Ah, there's hope for me, after all."

She playfully slugged his arm.

"Okay, my turn. Got a funny waitress story to share?"

She giggled. "When I first began work at the diner, this woman plops herself at the counter and asks if she could order a sandwich."

Zander grasped her hand. "Sounds normal to me."

"She then asks if the sandwich comes on bread."

"And you played the serious but polite waitress?"

"Definitely." She paused, again seeing the customer's wary eyes.

"I can tell you're leading to a *but*."

She smiled. He could already read her pretty well. "But when she asked if she could choose the sandwich bread or whether I'd force her to eat something she didn't like, I lost it."

"As in, explosive laughter?"

"I managed to excuse myself, rushed into the kitchen, and then doubled over in laughter. I don't normally do that kind of thing, but Caleb and I had just moved into our new apartment and I was totally focused on making a home and doing a good job at work. I forgot God was in control. This woman and the sandwich bit helped to loosen the tangles of tension."

"I hear you loud and clear. I was raised in a family who embraces God, but when my partner was killed and my injury robbed me of hope or possibly a career, I shrugged off God, figuring He didn't care about me. Until..."

Hope filled her as if it was a luscious summer day and warmth was sailing in on a gentle breeze through wide-open cabin windows. "Until what?"

"Until you came along."

Chapter 15

"Mama, if we have lights how come candles are lit?"

Jacey smiled at Caleb as Zander placed her dinner dish before her. Earlier, he'd found two candles and copper holders in a cupboard and suggested dining tonight by candlelight. "Yes, we have electricity. Zander not only cooked for us, but he's making this dinner nice with special touches, like candles."

Her son scrunched his face. "Zander?"

"Yes, buddy?"

"You're doing a very, very good job making it nice."

"Thanks, my friend."

Caleb giggled. "Mama, Zander called me his friend."

"I heard." Jacey reached for her guys' hands. "I'm glad he's our friend."

They said grace then dug into the hamburgers and corn-on-the-cob. Jacey groaned happily. "This is delicious, Z."

"I'm no gourmet cook, but I can do a few basics."

"Like barbeque?"

He smirked. "If driving to a barbeque joint and ordering the sloppiest dish on the menu counts, well, yeah, I can grill."

"You're funny." Jacey finished the last mouthful of her burger. She glanced out the front window. Christmas was the day after tomorrow. She'd hoped to be in sunny Florida at her friend's by now, a fresh beginning for both she and her son. Who would have imagined getting caught in a blizzard meant meeting an extraordinary man and a caring, gracious couple? From what could have been a dark time in her life came goodness and mercy. At this very moment, the setting sun's peace blanketed her surroundings, and a new tomorrow awaited not only her, but also her son and this gentleman named Zander.

74

Silent night. Holy night. All is calm. All is bright.

A tender touch came upon her shoulder.

"Jacey?"

She loved how her name sounded on his lips. "Yeah," she said softly. "Just thinking."

"I promised Caleb a bedtime story. Want to listen? It will be cheery."

"Absolutely." Wouldn't want to be anywhere else.

"AH, I HAVE THE PERFECT story just for you, Caleb."

From his pillow, the sleepy-eyed boy glanced up at Zander. "What's it about?"

"One day a grumpy clockmaker visited all the children in town." He continued the tale how the crotchety man got the children to behave for Santa. When a little snore snuck from the child's mouth, Zander smiled at Jacey.

"This is a special moment," he said softly.

"What is?"

"Telling bedtime stories to a little boy who wants to listen to me." He lifted Jacey's hand to his lips and gave it a kiss. "And watching his mom smile."

She motioned toward the cabin's main room and he nodded. She stood first, but he reached for her hand and together they tiptoed out of the room.

The dinner candles burned low and they sat on the sofa with the lone end table light on.

Jacey inched closer to him. "I'm glad you're better. I hated to see you in pain."

He opened his mouth but she pressed her finger against his lips.

"Don't deny it, Z."

He squeezed his eyes shut for a moment then opened them. "I won't. I need to level with you about things."

She tensed, and he absorbed her anguish.

"Don't worry," he said in an attempted soothing voice. "I like what we have going between us, like it's natural. Are you feeling it too?"

She nodded. "I am. But once the roads are cleared, probably tomorrow I'm figuring, we're heading in two different directions." She leaned forward, putting her head into her palms. Slowly, she dragged them down her pretty face. "I look around this cabin and think, wow, this is the coziest place I've ever lived in. Crazy, right? It's just two rooms except I'm nestled with you and my son under its protective roof. Yet, it's the first place I've ever fallen asleep and risen the next day convinced there's a chance for a happily ever after for me." She stood and went to the window to peer into the dark night. "But it's on borrowed time."

Within seconds he stood behind her, pulling her into his arms. "It's not crazy, Jacey. It's like the three of us are meant to be."

"We hardly know squat about each other." She sniffled. "I'm homeless, going south to my friend's. And you're heading north, to one of your parents' apartments."

"Well, we could change things." He ran his fingers through her hair, adoring how her blonde wispy locks curled toward her chin. How, when she smiled, she could illuminate the darkest of nights. How, with the feathery whisper of the letter Z for his name, she made it sound as if she was intimately familiar with him. This woman made the present count, not the past with its horrors and edgy corners.

"Jacey"—he kissed the tender side of her neck—"you know, I love saying your name." He gave her a moment for that to sink in. "We can both settle down in our new places, visit and get to know each other better. Then, if things continue well, and they will, we'll become Mr. and Mrs. Right and begin a new and better chapter in our lives with Caleb."

"And Samson?"

"Of course, Samson."

"I love your name too, Zander. It's wild but sturdy." She turned, resting her chin against his. "Just like you. I love those qualities in a man, spontaneous but steady." She wrapped her arms around his neck.

He took hold of her luscious lips with his and shared a kiss neither would ever forget. Or want to. Her body pressed against his, fitting snugly in all the right places. As he tightened his arms around her waist and spread his fingers across her lower back, she murmured delight. A thought crept into his mind. Not a trace of pain controlled his body. When he was with her the sun shined. Life was good.

They pulled apart.

Deep furrows crossed her brow. Something wasn't adding up.

"Out with it, Jacey. Tell me."

She grasped his hand and held it between them, near their hearts. "I don't know all about you. Like your last name. It's been either Zander or Z."

"And you've been Jacey. Fabulous Jacey. Super Jacey. And most definitely gorgeous Jacey. But I don't know your last name either, not that it matters."

A goofy but loving grin stretched her lips. He wanted to kiss it off.

He smiled. "What are you thinking?"

"What happens if you have an ugly last name?"

"Good thing I know you're teasing."

She stepped back a couple of inches and hugged her middle. "But seriously, what is your last name? Mine is Tucker. It's actually my maiden name. I switched back after my divorce."

"Paxton is mine, and proud of it. I'm the fifth generation of Paxtons in Pennsylvania."

Her mouth dropped open. A long shriek escaped. She glanced at the bedroom where her son slept, then back at him.

"I don't think you woke Caleb. What's wrong?"

She wrapped her arms around her middle as if she might fall apart. "Zander, who is your father?"

He rubbed the side of his head. "Why's my dad an issue?"

"Who is your father?" she repeated.

"A good man, liked by everyone in town. Bill Paxton."

"Married to June Paxton?"

A sharp pain twisted the back of his neck. This couldn't be good.

"Yes. We're talking about my mom and dad. They're really nice and I think you'll grow fond of them when . . ." He didn't like the disbelief clouding her eyes.

She backed away a few inches. "Let me guess the rest. June and Bill Paxton have a bunch of apartments they rent out and one is coincidentally available just for you. And this apartment happens to be located two miles down the road from Rick's Diner."

He gulped, his throat dry and scratchy. "And you know this why?"

"Bill Paxton was my landlord. He evicted Caleb and me from our apartment apparently so you could move in and continue with the rest of your life. In my eyes, he's heartless. You'd even called him a creep when you didn't know him by name. He has quite a few apartments waiting for occupation, places where he could have easily invited you to settle down. Instead, he kicks us out five days before Christmas because it's a nice, large place."

She stared at him, her bright eyes now dark. Sadness fringed her face. "Right before I met you, Zander, I fought to keep out of the rut of despair. Determined to find a home and a new beginning for both my son and me, I reined in the last scrap of optimism I could muster."

"And, then I came along . . . and ruined it?"

She shook her head. "No, don't you get it? You came along and reversed everything for me." She palmed the sides of her head. "I'm falling for you, Zander. As in love. The past few days were the most exciting and scariest days of my life. I didn't want to trust anyone again, but then you came along. I figured if God united us, then it's meant to be because He knows what He's doing." A little smile crept across her face then faded fast.

Had she really smiled? What was happening here?

"Call me silly, Zander, but I've come to imagine our meeting was God's Christmas gift to me and Caleb."

He moved toward her. She stepped back.

"Jacey, you're not silly. You're the loveliest woman ever, both inside and out. If anything, I'm thinking you're my Christmas gift from God. And yes, you heard correctly. You've opened my heart and mind to God again." He wanted to reach out to her and pull her into his arms, but was afraid she'd bolt. Instead, he shoved his hands into his jean pockets. "Tell me what you're thinking."

"I respect you and won't come between you and your family. We can't be together. It won't work." She lowered her head.

Seconds ago he wanted to hold her until the sadness went away. But how could he when it was he, and his family, that had spoiled every good possibility between them?

"I'm turning in for the evening," Jacey said. "I need a nice long chat with my Heavenly Father." She rushed toward the bedroom. When she reached the door, she paused and faced him. "With God's grace, tomorrow the roads will be cleared, businesses open, and I can rent a car to take us to sunny Florida." She slipped into the room, closing the door with a loud click.

Chapter 16

Jacey woke early the next morning, dressed, kissed her sleeping son, and tiptoed out of the bedroom. She carefully made her way across the cabin's main area. One glance at Zander sprawled on the sofa confirmed he was still asleep. Good. She needed fresh air and alone time.

Samson stood from his spot beside his sleeping master, stretched, and trotted over to her.

"Morning, buddy," she mouthed. She smiled despite the confusion tightening her chest. "You can come too."

Her winter coat and gray knit hat didn't stop the bone-chilling cold from wrapping around her like an unpleasant memory. Fresh drifts covered parts of the porch. She swooshed aside a pile of snow and sat on the top step. Samson plopped beside her and pressed tight against her side. Hugging her knees for warmth, she stared in the direction of the road, the place where her encounter with Z first happened four short days ago.

If someone had told her Tuesday morning, after receiving first the eviction notice and then the termination at work, that she'd literally crash into a man she wanted to spend the rest of her life with, she would have laughed. Zander, along with Joe, might have helped extricate her and Caleb from the car and saved their lives, but it wasn't a caped fantasy hero who'd occupied her mind and heart the past few days. Rather, she'd fallen for a gentle man, a funny man, one who remained calm in the face of danger. He faced his own pain and problems without self-pity. It wasn't easy, but he kept moving forward. Most importantly, he had accepted God back into his heart these past few days. Because of her? The idea she could have that magnitude of sway over one person—especially the one who had an equally huge impact on her—boggled her mind.

She petted Samson between the ears. "What do you think, buddy? Family is precious and I can't come between a man and his parents." She groaned. "I know what it's like not to have love and support. Zander and I must go our separate ways. It was just lousy coincidence that we met. I was foolish to imagine that God brought us together."

Samson whimpered and thumped his tail heavily.

"What is it?" She followed the animal's gaze straight ahead and almost smiled at the three deer, one strutting as the leader with the other two following through the thick snow as easily as if on a summer stroll across a grassy pasture. She let out a tight breath.

Samson nudged his snout against her leg and whined.

She petted him again. "Hush. Let's not wake anyone."

The determined dog pawed at her leg.

"Are you trying to tell me to stay?" The tall pine trees creaked in the wind with its heavy snow cover. Another gust brought woodstove smoke from the Billings' house. Images flashed in her mind. Of family gatherings before a Christmas tree. Gardening vegetables. Playing Frisbee with her son and . . . She sighed. "I'm going to miss this place. It's kind of magical. It sure would make a cozy home."

Samson let out a little woof.

"Ah, you agree. Sorry, boy. And I'm going to miss you . . . and how I'll miss Zander. But, I know what it's like to hurt because of an estrangement in one's family and I won't do that to him by coming between him and his loving parents. One way or the other, today Caleb and I will leave without him." She blinked back tears. "And without you, Samson."

"No, Mama."

Jacey whipped her head around. Caleb stood at the door. Dressed in Joe's borrowed flannel shirt he'd worn as PJs, along with his jeans and boots, he grasped a blanket in hand. He hadn't carried a protective blankie since he'd turned three.

Samson propelled right toward her son.

"Sweetheart, we're going to leave for Florida soon."

"No, Mama." He stamped his foot. "We don't leave without Zander and Samson."

She rallied a tiny smile. "Let's get you fully dressed. It's time to continue our adventure and have ourselves a merry Christmas."

"With Zander and Samson?"

"No, honey. We have to—"

Caleb bolted off the porch and raced across the field toward Aubrey and Joe's. Samson took off after him.

"Caleb," Jacey shouted. She jumped up and was about to run after him when she heard her name called. She turned around. Zander.

Concern arched his brows and widened his eyes. In two strides, he stood beside her.

"Caleb—"

"I saw. I heard." He grabbed her hand. "Let's go."

Together. She was grateful.

They paused minutes later behind Caleb and Samson, who now stood on the Billings' porch.

Caleb lifted his hand to knock, but the door pulled open from the inside. Zander hooked elbows with Jacey to keep her from moving closer.

"Joe," Caleb said as if he'd seen his best friend. "You're in your PJs like me."

"I am." Joe shook his tall self from his bathrobe and wrapped it over Caleb's shoulders. "No sense in getting cold." He glanced at Jacey and Zander then back at Caleb. "Does your mama know where you are?"

Caleb shrugged. "Mama said we're gonna leave today. Without Zander and Samson."

"And you're not happy about that?"

Aubrey appeared beside her husband and smiled at Caleb.

"No. I like Zander. I like Samson. He's like a daddy."

"Samson's like a daddy?" Joe said, his voice thick in tease.

"You're silly, Joe. Zander's like a daddy. And Mama likes him. A lot."

As Zander wrapped an arm around Jacey and pulled her tight against his side, she exhaled a breath she didn't realize she'd held.

"Then why the sad face, Caleb?"

"Because Zander and Samson will go bye-bye forever. I heard Mama. She doesn't want to hurt Zander."

Jacey pressed a knuckle against her lips. Her poor baby.

Zander lifted her chin. Her gaze met his. She didn't want to turn away from him again. Ever.

"But we need a house," Caleb added. "Zander too. Can we live with you?"

"Oh, my." Aubrey stepped forward and patted Caleb's cheeks. She peeked at Jacey and Zander and raised her voice. "Joe and I have talked about selling our cabin and two acres of land. This might be the perfect time. With a little fixing and expanding, the cabin can become home sweet home."

Hope opened in Jacey's heart like a blossom in spring sunshine. Spring. One season away from winter.

Joe winked at his wife. "We can talk to Jacey and Zander about it."

"Yay," Caleb squealed. "They can be Mama and Daddy."

Aubrey slipped her arm around Joe's. "Yes, marriage is a lovely way to spend happily ever after."

"Like in my storybooks?"

"Exactly," Aubrey said. "Come inside, Caleb. I'm making hot cocoa."

"I love cocoa." Jacey's little boy zipped indoors without a glance over his shoulder to see whether his new grandmotherly friend followed.

Zander framed his hands around Jacey's face. "Will you marry me, Jacey? Today or tomorrow or in a short while. We'll work out the details. I just want to live with you, no matter where we call home. Our families will have to respect us. And we'll have to respect them."

"Yes, Z. I can't imagine it any other way." She let her happy tears flow down her cheeks. "This is the best Christmas I've ever had." She glanced upward. "Thank you, God."

She smiled at Zander and their lips met for delicious taste. She expected many more kisses to follow.

"Hey, you two lovebirds," Joe called from the porch.

They glanced up.

He pointed a finger behind them, up the rise of the hill and toward the cabin that could be seen above the grove of trees. "I forgot all about this until just now."

Red, green, and silver lights twinkled. Christmas lights. They must have been covered from the falling snow. Now they sparkled as if Santa had flown over the cabin with his sleigh.

"Merry Christmas, my friends." Joe grasped Aubrey's hand and they both let out a hearty *ho ho ho*.

"And Merry Christmas to you," Jacey and Zander said. Together.

Note from the Author

I hope you've enjoyed Jacey and Zander's story, *And You Came Along*. I love writing stories that fuse together romance, family drama, and faith in a clean fiction style. Stories of second chances and renewed hope against the odds tug at my heart. When I began to create a story set in the middle of a blizzard, the union of Jacey and Zander immediately came to mind, centered on the challenge of whether or not true love is ever mistaken and rising above difficult situations. If you enjoyed their story I'd love to hear from you!

http://www.elainestock.com/contact.

http://www.elainestock.com/signup.

About the Author

ELAINE STOCK IS THE author of *Always With You*, which released in January 2016 and has won the 2017 Christian Small Publishers Association Book of the Year Award in fiction. Her novels fuse romance, family drama and faith in a clean fiction style. She is a member of American Christian Fiction Writers, Romance Writers of America, and Women's Fiction Writers Association, and contributes to the international "Happy Sis Magazine" and "InD'tale Magazine." In addition to Twitter, Facebook, and Goodreads, she hangs out on her active six-year-old blog, Everyone's Story, dedicated to uplifting and encouraging all readers through the power of story and hope.

Elaine's short story, *In His Own Time*, won the People's Choice Award in the FamilyFiction Contest and has been published in a printed anthology: The Story: 2014 Anthology. Her short story *The Forever Christmas Gift* is published in the Amazon bestseller Christmas Treasures: A Collection of Christmas Stories.

Born in Brooklyn, NY, Elaine has now been living in upstate, rural New York with her husband for more years than her stint as a NYC gal.

She enjoys long walks down country roads, visiting New England towns, and of course, a good book.

Find Elaine At:

Website: http://elainestock.com
Everyone's Story Blog: http://elainestock.com/blog
Twitter: http://www.twitter.com/ElaineStock
Facebook: https://www.facebook.com/AuthorElaineStock
Goodreads: http://goodreads.com/ElaineStock

Other Books by the Author:

ALWAYS WITH YOU:

In the heart of the Adirondacks, Isabelle lives in the shadow of a dark family secret whose silent burden strips her family of emotional warmth and faith in God. Tyler belongs to the religious sect called The Faithful. When families and values collide, they marry and believe they're on the right track for happiness. But, when the truth comes out, Isabelle faces two choices: Staying could endanger her child. Leaving could cost her life.

LOOK FOR ELAINE STOCK'S next full-length novel, **Her Good Girl**, a coming of age story of a whole family to release in January 2018.